CRITICAL ACCL...
WATER FOR DRO...

A This Is Horror Publication
www.ThisIsHorror.co.uk

ISBN: 978-0-9575481-7-6

First published in Great Britain in 2014 by This Is Horror

Editor-in-Chief: Michael Wilson
Cover/Design: Pye Parr

Printed in Great Britain

WATER FOR DROWNING

RAY CLULEY

THIS IS HORROR

AUTHOR'S INTRODUCTION

I STARTED 'WATER For Drowning' around the end of 2013 as a way of dealing with a mermaid obsession that began in my teens. I blame my college lecturer. He told me that in literature the mermaid is often a symbol of sexual frustration and this had quite an impact on me (I was a teenager at the time, remember; I could relate). So that's where it started. This was followed by discovering a very non-Disney version of Andersen's 'The Little Mermaid' which developed my interest thanks to the poor girl's all-consuming desire and willingness to suffer for someone she loves. I got over that pretty quick and moved on to mermaids as femme fatales. Much sexier. As siren seductress of the sea, mermaids now held a very strong, very different (and very complicated) appeal for me. 'Water For Drowning' is meant to be the story that gets it all out of my system.

The story began life as a single image that came to me in the bath (too much information?), an image which gave me a scene to use in the story and, more importantly, introduced me to Genna. You'll know the scene when you get to it, I expect. It's often this way for me, the story beginning as a single idea or visual image which either connects with other ideas I've had or shapes itself into something on the page as I write draft zero (the draft no one ever sees but me). And come to think of it, these ideas and images will often arrive while I'm in the bath or shower; perhaps the water has some special creative power…

Initially I intended to write from Genna's perspective but it didn't quite work. Her story was too familiar when told directly, and besides, I wanted her to remain distant as a character. I also wanted to try something a little different so that instead of the usual 'bad stuff happening to good people' approach typical of the genre, I had something good happen to someone bad. Well, maybe 'bad' is too strong. Unpleasant. I didn't like Josh much, not at first, but as unpleasant as he can be I had a lot of fun with his voice. He's not me. He's definitely not me. But he is *kinda* someone I know. In fact, I know (or rather *knew*) a few people like the ones you'll meet here, so I suppose some thanks should go to them for the inspiration. Not by name, though. I didn't like them that much.

While I'm on the subject of thanks, there are a few others who deserve a mention.

The most important is V. H. Leslie. She deserves an ocean of gratitude for always being my first reader (and sometimes a second as well) and for being such a positive influence in my life and on my writing. When life gives you lemons, she'll do tequila shots with you. So thanks, Tori. As always.

Thanks also go to Pye Parr for some absolutely stunning artwork. It's beautiful. It's *perfect*. Personally I'd buy this book just for the cover. He's done great work on other This is Horror chapbooks too, by the way, and each is well worth reading.

When I started 'Water For Drowning' it was entirely with This is Horror in mind, but during the writing process I discovered the chapbook series was coming to an end. Still, I carried on (the story had a firm hold by then) and, as fate would have it, an invite came out of the blue to contribute to the chapbook line anyway. I was delighted to be able to say, "I have just the thing" without, you know, lying, just as I am delighted to be a part of such a strong series of stories. So this is me, landing the one I thought got away. All of which is a rather long-winded way of saying thanks, as well, to This is Horror.

Regarding my influences and inspirations, 'Water For Drowning' follows in the wake of various sources. 'The Little Mermaid', of course, as I've mentioned. Thanks Mr Andersen. I've upset many a student in telling them the 'true' story and now I get to write my own anti-Disney version of the mermaid myth. A stanza from T.S. Eliot's masterpiece

'The Love Song of J. Alfred Prufrock' was also important. It gave me the title for a previous story, 'I Have Heard the Mermaids Singing', but I've not stolen any lines this time. I can't say the same thing for Josh. Speaking of Josh, a wonderful poem called 'Anchor Baby' by Tim Burton was a hugely important inspiration here. It comes from a great collection called *The Melancholy Death of Oyster Boy* which I thoroughly recommend. Add to these the film *Splash*, numerous wonderful paintings, and even an old leaflet about 'Mr Harry Phillips' Mermaid' at the Brighton Aquarium, and you have all the grit I tried to form a pearl around.

Anyway, the short version is I like mermaids and I'm thankful to various people, but enough of all that. I can hear the surf rolling in, and with it a distant voice, singing.

On with the story...

Ray Cluley,
June 2014

I FIRST SAW Genna at one of our Isle of Wight gigs. She seemed normal. Gothed-up to fuck and off her face, but normal. We were playing cover stuff, nothing wild, Stereophonics at the time, I think, me doing my best to add a bit of Kelly gravel and wondering where the fuck the rest of my beer had gone because my throat was gonna need it. Genna, who I didn't know was Genna yet, was bouncing around at the front of the crowd and any minute now her tits were going to come up out of her top. I didn't have a fucking clue then how screwed up she was, and at the time I wouldn't have cared anyway. You could've said Josh, mate, she's a fucking loon, wants to be a mermaid one day, and I'd have said so what, as long as she doesn't stink of fish.

We finished 'My Own Worst Enemy' and went into some Oasis bollocks and then we got darker with Nirvana and some old school Stones. Same shit everybody knows but it paid the bills, sort of, and girls love whatever you play. And that's what it was all about – the girls. Anyone in a band who says different is bullshitting you because *you're* a girl and they wanna stick their dick in you somewhere. Bands play and girls drool in their knickers and that's how it was, except for Hench who I'm still pretty sure is gay even if he did fuck Beth's sister.

"You're serenading that ginger bit," he yelled during the break. I could barely hear him over the Zeppelin, which was a bit mum and dad for me but good enough for a beer break.

"She ain't ginger," I said, "that's some bottled stop-light colour."

He shrugged and I swear he checked out the barman.

"She with anybody?" I asked him.

Hench cupped his hand around his ear so I leant over, spilling my pint, and shouted, "She with anyone? The ginger?"

He looked around for her so I punched his chest to get his attention again. If it hadn't been so rammed in there he'd have probably fallen over because I think I was a bit enthusiastic about it. "Not *now*, you fuckin' idiot. I don't mean is she with anybody *now*. Is she a band aid?"

Hench shrugged. "Don't think so." Then he nudged me and said, "Not yet," and winked, which only confirmed he was a gaylord.

Genna wasn't a groupie, as it happens. She was fit and all that, nice tits, like I said, tights that were all ladders where it mattered (which was around the thighs), but she didn't hang about after the gig. Not that first one, anyway.

First one I saw her at, I mean, not first one we ever played. We were pretty good by then, getting regular work, a decent fan base. Break N' Wave, you might've heard of us? I wanted to call us Breaking Wave, be a bit less Guns N' Roses, but Tommy said no so all the other fuckwit followers said no as well in case he quit or something. He's a fucking cock, but there you go.

"Redhead?" he asked as I shrugged back into my guitar. He nodded without me answering and said her name was Genna because Tommy fucking knows everybody in the world apparently.

"Good shag?" I asked him, just in case. If the cunt had been there already I would've left her well alone. I didn't want his sloppy seconds.

But the bastard started in with a 'Tainted Love' that was more Manson than Soft Cell and I had to get to the mic without knowing the answer.

She was gone by the time we packed up.

ABOUT A WEEK after that gig, one of Kate's friends was having a party – Selina or Semelina or fucking Xena or something – and we were all there and more than a bit wasted. It was a tame one really, lots of drinking and lots of pot but only Muse and Snow Patrol, shit like that. Nothing wrist-slittin' like Coldplay, thank fuck, but I was sure that if I waited around long enough we'd get some. That, or fucking Damien Rice or something. Good stuff, all right, okay, but not exactly party material. If it turned into Portishead I was fucking leaving.

Anyway, Tommy had his tongue down Kate's throat, trying to suck out her larynx or something with one hand under her skirt as if it might try to escape that way. Vince had his arms around two birds on the sofa, saying something wise and profound no doubt, being as neither of them was much older than sixteen. One girl, Sam, was making Hench uncomfortable by putting her hand where his cock should've been. I was so stoned I nearly told her she had the right name (and the right chest actually) but nothing between the legs he'd like, spluttering a laugh even though I hadn't actually said it.

"What's so funny?" asked the blonde who'd been trying to get my attention. She was wearing a top too short for her, the kind designed to show off the midriff which is only sexy if you don't have a belt of blubber instead of a waist. She'd pressed her tits against my arm too many times to count but I knew from Tommy that she didn't so much have the clap as the whole fucking applause. She probably got it from Vince who thought safe sex was scanning for viruses after downloading porn.

Someone handed me a joint, though I could've sworn I'd just passed it, and Vince said, "Josh wants to fuck a ginger, *that's* pretty funny." He was squeezing at one of the sofa girls, turning his body so the other couldn't see, keeping his options open.

"Twat," I said, and threw something at him which turned out to be a bottle which turned out to miss, smashing somewhere in the kitchen. Still, herpes girl backed off. Probably wondering where she could get a ginger wig or something.

"She's not ginger," said Hench, "she's traffic-light bottle." Which everyone seemed to find hysterical.

"Isle of Wight gig?" Kate asked. Tommy tried to pull her face back around but she held him off for a minute.

"Genna," Tommy said for me. "Yeah." He was probably hoping that would end it and he could get back to sucking up Kate's insides, but she laughed and turned away from him even more.

"She's fucking nuts, mate," she told me. "Tried to drown herself."

"Right."

"No shit."

She must've meant it because she was pulling a strap back up and hiding the lacy bra we'd all seen already. She took a puff on the joint coming around and said in a voice of held breath, "In a bowl of fucking cornflakes or something," before releasing the smoke.

"It was a bowl of water," Tommy said. "She put salt in it."

"How do you know that?" Kate asked.

Tommy shrugged. "Just do."

"Anyway, she's not right," Kate said. "I've talked to her a few times and she sounds like a fucking Tori Amos song."

"She *looks* like a Tori Amos song," Tommy said, and Kate slapped his arm, though I don't think even Tommy knew what he meant.

"You don't know shit," Kate said.

"I know she didn't drown in her fucking breakfast cereal."

"And how do you know what she has for breakfast?"

Which wasn't exactly the logical next question but we were drunk and stoned and Kate's a woman so what the fuck's logic got to do, got to do with it? But then Hench started singing, "Never was a cornflake girl," and suddenly we were all laughing and forgetting what we were talking about.

Kate put Tommy's hands on her tits again to show him everything was okay and then chased his tongue with hers for a minute before dragging him away. Must've been one of those rare occasions when they wanted privacy, so they went upstairs. She waved at me as they went.

A little bit about Kate and Tommy. Kate's a very good looking girl but she's only playing at grungy; smoky grey eye shadow and a pierced tongue but that's it. She talks about getting her clit done but never does. Talks about tats, doesn't get any. She's also one of those pretty girls that doesn't like other pretty girls. Anyway, she's as much a part of the band as you can be without playing a fucking instrument, unless sucking Tommy's cock counts. Usually her idea of privacy is to close her eyes if others are around but sometimes she'll take Tommy to a different room. Even then they rarely shut the door.

I saw them fucking once. Kate was riding him hard in reverse cowgirl and didn't seem to care that I saw. She even moved her hair away so I could see her tits. I fucked her myself not long after that. Tommy had been doing her and then he went out to fetch a takeaway or whatever and I went into his room pretending to look for something. Kate was still panting from their session and made some joke about seconds, so I swept the quilt back to call her bluff. She was completely naked but all she did was laugh so what was I supposed to do? Tommy never found out, best I can tell. Not that any of us treat a girl like she's going to meet the parents or anything. Plenty more fish in the sea and all that. We were pretty fucking good together, Kate and me, but sometimes I think she only did it to get one over on Tommy. Sometimes I think I did, too.

It's not that I hate Tommy, it's just the guy's a complete prick. He thinks he's fucking God's gift because he knows everyone and they all seem to like him. Plus he has this annoying habit of calling music legends by their first names, like they're his best buddies or something. David instead of Bowie, Mick instead of Jagger, can you believe that shit? True even if you don't. And *Kurt*. Fuckin' Kurt, *all* the time. I never really got the Cobain thing myself. Jagger, yeah – there's a guy who's put his dick in some good looking girls – but Cobain? We got Tommy a 'What Would Kurt Do?' t-shirt once to take the piss but he loved it. He laughed and said, "Shoot himself," and we pretty much pissed our pants. The joke's old now but he still wears it to every gig. He changes afterwards though, like he's only playing at being in a band. Puts glasses on and a fresh shirt like he's Clark Kent or something. Clark Cunt.

Anyway, he was upstairs fucking Kate and I was downstairs sitting in a haze of dope-smoke wondering, 'What would Kurt do?' and thinking 'Shoot himself' and asking, "Anyone got the ginger's number?"

* * *

IN THE END, I got it from Vince. I didn't want to know how he had it, but he must've guessed my concern because he said, "Never tried her myself," adding he would if I rated her. "I'd lick the shit-grit from her dirt hole," was his exact phrase. He has a way with words, Vince. Not a nice way, but entirely his. Anyway, I sent a text that didn't seem too keen. Just the details of our next gig, a Portsmouth one, local. She text back saying she was already going. Didn't ask who I was, didn't bother with a smiley face or a kiss or anything, so I left it at that and waited for Friday.

She was early, standing at the bar as we set up. I played it cool, barely even looked at her. She was wearing those shiny black leggings, you know, the ones that look permanently wet or like they've just been painted on, and they were low on her hips. Tucked into the top was a hip flask. First one I've actually seen on someone's hip. And she had this tight torn t-shirt riding high thanks to her tits. Something sparkled in her bellybutton and something else arched over it, maybe a dolphin, which was a bit lame but not a lay-breaker. She was stirring her drink with a straw and making a whirlpool of the ice cubes.

All right, maybe it wasn't exactly a quick look.

"Something for the wank bank?" Vince asked, nudging me out of the way as he struggled past with an amp.

"Fuck yourself, Vince."

"Guaranteed satisfaction." He put the amp down and got in the way of me putting mine next to it, sidestepping left, right, left.

"Fuck sake, stop being a–"

He took the amp from me and said, "Just get the beers in," nodding more towards Genna than the bar, so I let him off being a twat.

Being on her own made it much easier, no friends to navigate with all their questions and tests and that bullshit girls do. "Hey, Genna, long time."

"You don't know me," she said. "You just know my name."

Which kinda took the wind outta my sails – abandon ship, Mayday, Mayday – and usually I would've said something cutting, like everybody knows your name, it's on the toilet walls or something, but she'd said it with such a sparkle in her eyes that I was hooked and stuck around for another go.

"Yeah, your ex told me," I said, pointing vaguely to the rest of the band. It was pretty fucking vague because they were scattered around everywhere.

"No exes," Genna said. "No boyfriends, either, before you try tacking that course. Just me and my maelstrom." She twirled her finger around the side of her head and that should have been my first clue, that and the word maelstrom, but how was I to know she was being honest? How was I supposed to know she was actually fucking mental?

"You gonna play 'Coastline'?" she asked.

That surprised me. We were playing our own stuff this time and our own stuff was pretty fucking good. Better than most of the other crap out there, anyway, though I suppose that's not saying much. And she already seemed to know the songs.

"'Coastline'," I said. "Sure. Any other requests?"

She smiled. "Not yet. Ask me again later."

I nodded and took the beers back to the band.

It was a fucking good gig. We opened with 'Mariner's Song' and I scanned the room, checking for anyone better but ending up back at Genna just like I knew I would. A couple of the others looked good for a go but there was something special about Genna. I dunno. Maybe the way she moved to the song – *my* song, I wrote the fucking thing – her eyes closed, body almost lazy.

We did 'Crossfire Girl' next, which is lighter but faster with a chorus that's quick to pick up. Sure enough she sang along with the crowd, but she surprised me by joining in with some of the verses too. When we did 'The Uninvited', which is pretty much Nirvana without actually being Nirvana, she glanced my way a couple of times. I don't think she liked that one because she frowned a lot, but maybe it was just the lyrics. She retreated back to the bar during that one. After that I improvised, changing the set without warning into 'Wild-Water Woman' and forcing the others to catch up. Tommy was pissed off because he had to change guitars quickly but it was the right thing to do: the crowd loved it. And so did Genna, which was the main thing. She pushed back into the masses, drawn by the thrumming rhythms, and she let them sweep her along, swaying and rocking to the eddies and swells of the song, losing herself in the waves of our music.

We played better that night than we had in a long time. Each song washed into the next and nobody fucked up. Hench beat his kit like he was a fucking octopus, Vince managed his solos with a kind of casual modesty that was unusual for him but way more effective than any of his usual grandstanding, and Tommy backed up my vocals without hogging the strongest lines. Me, I didn't so much sing as let the words pour out in whatever way they wanted, and they pretty much poured out perfect. The crowd fucking loved it, but better than that, *we* fucking loved it, which hadn't been the case for quite a while. We shared a lot of happy looks, steered the way into fresh riffs and new rhythms with eye contact, and grinned like we were fucking gods.

Genna loved every second of it. She never went back to the bar (though I saw her take a few nips from that hip flask), didn't leave to piss or smoke, just let every song turn her around, move her up, move her down, hold her in its tide. When we played 'Coastline' she practically came, and she danced in a way that made me want to as well. She started the encore when the set was done and we ended up doing three more, playing 'Sally' (which I nearly changed to Genna but thank-fuckfully didn't), 'Snow Chamber', and then 'Rye-Catcher' to bring the whole thing to a frenetic finish. I wrote that one off my face and still don't quite know what it means, but with Vince leading us in and then trailing out like a dying heartbeat, it doesn't really matter what the words mean anyway.

After the gig we were so high on the performance that we left our kit and had a few drinks. I was taking a pint from Vince, reaching out over the crowded bar, when Genna came over. She leaned in close so I could hear and yelled, "Great set!" I felt her breasts against my arm and chest and thought, yeah, you too, putting my hand on her waist to keep her close. Her skin was damp with sweat but smooth and cool.

"What do you want?" I asked her. I meant to drink, but the hurt on her face told me she'd heard different so I quickly added, "Beer? Wine? The hard stuff? Get something fancy, Vince is paying for once." She looked pleased or relieved or whatever and took my pint so I signalled for another which Vince promptly handed over before leaving us to it. He's the least twatish in the band, really, but then maybe I was just still flying high from the performance.

"We played 'Coastline'," I said.

"I noticed. Thanks."

"Any other requests now?"

She smiled, drank some beer, and said, "It's your turn; I owe you for the song."

She was testing me, seeing how quick I'd go for something sleazy. Usually I'd have done exactly that, and usually sleazy works, thank you very much, but I was liking the game; there was no need to reel her in just yet.

"How about your phone number?"

"You've already got it."

My text could have been from anyone but somehow she knew.

"We could grab something to eat?"

She checked the time on her phone and downed the rest of her drink. It was impressive. "If we're quick, I know just the place."

She watched me, waiting. I drank down the rest of my pint and put the glass down in the rough direction of the bar, not caring if I reached. "Just let me tell the guys." I wanted to make sure someone took care of my stuff if I wasn't back before kick out.

Genna took my hand and pulled me through the crowd behind her. I grabbed Tommy's shoulder as I passed and said I'd be back in a bit.

"Whatever, man. I've sorted a lock-in so just come back here afterwards." He glanced at Genna then said to me, "Good luck, mate."

We pushed our way through a tide of people heading in the opposite direction and emerged outside into a cloud of cigarette smoke. Genna pulled a face and waved it away and I made a mental note not to spark up in front of her.

"Where to?"

She still had my hand, pulling me across the road and forcing cars to stop to let us by. Taxis, mostly, entirely used to the nightlife that strolled across their path.

"The beach," she said.

The beach was a fucking *result*. I wasn't thrilled by the idea of grit-dick or a sandy arse crack but I figured she'd be worth it.

"There's this place," Genna said. "Best fish and chips *ever*."

"Brilliant."

If she heard the sarcasm she pretended not to, and to be honest I was starving so it wasn't such a bad idea anyway. I could always get her onto the beach afterwards.

The next street took us down to the sea front. Genna took a deep breath through her nose and held it for a moment before letting it out of her mouth. "You've gotta love that smell," she said.

"Yeah, good sea breeze," I said, thinking if she wanted something romantic she was shit out of luck. I'm capable, I write songs for fuck's sake, but right then, looking at her closed eyes and taking in the tang of salty night air, I didn't feel like bullshitting her. There was a simplicity to what she said, what she did, how she did it, that wouldn't let me come up with any of the usual crap. Not here, where the surf was sweeping wet curves up the sand and stones.

"I love the sea," she said finally, opening her eyes to look at me. They were a gorgeous bright shining blue and I realised she gothed her eyes up dark the same way a painter used a frame to show off his work. Okay, I must've been a bit pissed to be thinking that way but she seemed a little drunk too, to be honest, though thinking back on it now I'm not so sure it was the alcohol. I think it was the soft hush of the sea as it came in, and then quietly receded. I think it was the salt you could taste if you breathed with your mouth open.

It was completely the wrong time to go in for a kiss, though Genna seemed to be waiting for *something*, so I said, "I love the sea too." I realised as I said it that it was actually true. I'd just never said it before.

"That's cool," she said. Then, "Do you believe in mermaids?"

*   *   *

GENNA TOLD ME quite a few stories about mermaids. Did you know the original Little Mermaid dies? Maybe everybody knows that, but I didn't. One minute she's living in her nice coral palace in a city of seaweed or something, you know, amber for windows and mussel shells on the roofs, whatever, and then there's a big fuck-off storm and a shipwreck and she falls in love with some prince and it all gets fucked up.

In this other story Genna told me, a man marries a mermaid or a selkie or undine or something (they're all pretty much the same) but then banishes her and marries someone normal. The first one, the mermaid, she comes back to kill him – she has to, for some reason, and it's the only time she's allowed back on land – but I can't remember how that one ends.

Anyway, she didn't tell me those stories then. She just talked about this thing in Brighton.

"You ever been?" she asked. We were walking slowly, eating our fish and chips.

"A few gigs."

"There's an awesome Sea Life Centre there," Genna said. "It used to have a mermaid. Back when it was Brighton Aquarium."

"Okay."

She'd reminded me of something. Something from a mostly forgotten conversation with Kate and Tommy, maybe. The bowl of salt water, swimming around in my mind and nearly close enough to remember. Or maybe it was a premonition I was feeling, like the reverse of déjà vu or something. Some sense of foreboding.

"Probably not a real mermaid," Genna said.

"Probably."

"We're talking, like, late eighteen hundreds or something and they'd fake all sorts of things back then. You know, stitch half a monkey corpse to a giant salmon and call it a mermaid. I remember this one, the Brighton one, because I've got one of the leaflets at home. Mr Harry

Phillips' Mermaid, and then a pencil drawing beneath, 'Half Beautiful Woman, Half Fish'." She looked at me, popped a chip in her mouth, and said, "She wasn't all that beautiful."

"And people believed it?"

She shrugged. "People will believe anything if it makes them happy. Even if they know it isn't real."

Later she told me all the different types. Mermaids are the classics. Half beautiful woman and half fish (and thank fuck it's that way around) reduced now to sailor tattoos or used on the covers of relaxation CDs. Then you've got your selkies and sirens and all sorts of other mythological creatures, each with their songs and dancing and other temptations, beautiful evil bitches and doomed lovers and sometimes both at the same time. Selkies are basically seals and, according to some, they're actually drowned people given new form. They're allowed to come back once a year, shedding their selkie seal skin to become human again, only they have to keep the skin safe because whoever holds the skin holds power over them. You can also call them ashore by crying into the sea or something. Sirens, they were originally these bird-like creatures luring ships onto rocks according to some old Greek story, but somewhere along the line they've become mixed in with mermaids. Genna told me it's probably because of something called a nix, a kind of mermaid that lives in rivers and lakes that would lure men to them by playing beautiful music or singing, though I'm pretty sure having their tits out helped. Then they'd drag the men into the water and drown them. There's a male version too who played the fiddle and did the same thing to women.

There are lots of mermaid stories, and lots of different versions of the same stories, but they're always about love. That's what Genna told me.

She was pretty fucked up, but she was right about that.

"SO WHERE IS she now?" Kate asked when I got back to the pub.

"Who?"

The guys laughed. Kate gave me her wicked smile. "Come on," she said, "where did you dump the body?"

I gave her the middle finger.

"Lovely," she said. "But I'm not smelling it."

I wasn't completely honest with them about what happened. I said something about getting my dick wet because it was kind of true and I took my high fives and back slaps. I didn't tell them it was because we'd gone swimming.

Not that I swam – Genna did, but not me. Supposed to leave it an hour anyway, aren't you, after eating? I said that to Genna when she suggested it but she only laughed. "Come on…"

"Now?"

People were still walking the esplanade and cars were passing – taxis mostly, and boy racers with their stereos whacked up to destroy whatever music they were playing. It wasn't club kick out time yet so it wasn't *that* busy, but busy enough.

"Yeah, now. Why not?"

"Because I don't want some fucker to nick my clothes."

"We can go in by the pier."

She meant the South Parade Pier. Her eyes were bright with the idea. It did mean we could hide our clothes and have a little privacy.

She could tell I'd agreed so she dashed off across the beach, shrieking in that way girls do to let you know you're supposed to chase them, which I did. I didn't want to miss her stripping off in the shadows.

As soon as we were underneath the pier, Genna pulled her top up and off and yanked her leggings down. I couldn't see her tits yet, she had her back to me, but bending down to unfasten her shoes gave me a great fucking view and then she was turning around in only her underwear.

"Hey, you too," she said. She hugged herself, arms across her chest, but I think more from the cold than any modesty. It wasn't enough to hide her tits anyway and they were just as great as I thought they'd be, even in a bra.

"Nice tattoos."

"Yeah, you were looking at those."

"I was."

I wasn't, but I did. She had lines around her thighs like garters that were actually rings of seaweed, if you can believe that. Seaweed even if you don't. And I finally noticed that the something diving over her bellybutton was not a lame-ass dolphin but a mermaid.

"You're still staring."

"You're still fucking gorgeous."

She laughed, which was a good sign. I stepped on the heels of my shoes to drag them off and Genna went running into the sea.

"Fuck."

I hurried out of my shirt and jeans and chased her.

It was fucking *freezing*. This country is not made for skinny-dipping, and leaving underwear on didn't help in the slightest. I swore at the cold as I splashed into the surf and tried to catch some air to breathe with. Genna, though, was leaping over the tiny waves as they came in as if on summer holiday and as soon as it was deep enough she dived *under*. I fucking well didn't. I just waded in, sucking in breaths as the water rose up over my thighs and higher. If Genna hadn't resurfaced right beside me I probably would've gone back. She grabbed me and pulled me close, laughing as I gasped at the water washing up over my waist, but I put my arms around her chilled body and we kissed in the dark ocean.

I could taste the sea on her lips and smell it on her skin. My hands were all over her, cupping her ass and holding her waist and stroking her back. Her skin was smooth, not goose-pimply at all, and she was completely serene whereas me, I was shivering like a spaz. I didn't care, though. When her hand dipped below the water and into the front of my shorts I said, "Remember it's cold," and she laughed.

"It's not the size of the wave," she said, "but the motion of the ocean."

"Yeah. It's not how deep you fish the water but how you wiggle your worm."

She laughed again. She had a great laugh. "Nice."

We kissed some more, her hand still in my shorts.

"You know when you're swimming in the sea," she said, "and the water goes suddenly cold?" We were still kissing between sentences. "When it goes *really* cold all of a sudden?" I made a noise for yes and she whispered into my ear. "That's water that's had death in it."

I moved away to look at her. Her hair was slicked back wet and the makeup had run from her eyes in dark streaks but she only looked more gorgeous. I didn't know how I was meant to respond but she saved me the trouble, coming close again to kiss my neck.

"One fish eats another fish," she murmured, "or the water fills someone's lungs and drowns them." She moaned as I touched her and said, "Cold water is water that's taken lives."

What the fuck was I supposed to say to that?

I went with, "Well this water's fucking freezing."

"Because it's the middle of the night," she said, "don't worry." She slipped her other hand into my shorts. Her bra was wet and see through and her nipples were hard and so was I because of how she looked and because of how she used her hands and because of how she looked and, *God*, she was good with her hands, all of which far outweighed any crazy shit she said about cold water.

"Sing me something," she said.

"Later."

I pulled at her underwear. The hand job was good, *really* fucking good, but I needed to be inside her.

"Sing me 'Coastline' or I'll stop."

So I did, and she didn't, and it was all so fucking weird and amazing that as the song finished I came in her hands.

"And that," she said afterwards, "Is how you make a mermaid." She smiled. "Think of all those fish you just impregnated."

It was a fucking crazy thing to say, but I laughed anyway. Sort of.

"I get so thirsty whenever I come here," she said, and sighed. Then she dipped down so the sea came up over her chin, opened her mouth, and drank a shit-load of seawater. I definitely saw her swallow.

"Genna, Jesus."

"What?" She'd cupped some water into her hands and offered it to me.
"No thanks."
"Why not?"

Because it's fucking seawater, I wanted to say. And because it's got my come in it, for fuck's sake.

She drank it happily enough, though. Which was when I thought, fuck, she really is mental.

Of course, I didn't tell the guys in the pub any of that.

I'VE RESEARCHED SEAWATER a bit since then. About how drinking it makes you crazy. It doesn't, apparently. That's just a myth. You know, like mermaids.

It does fuck your blood pressure, which can put too much pressure on your heart. The heart rate goes right up and breathing quickens. And it can impair judgement. But then I didn't drink any of that shit and I had some of those symptoms too by the end.

Mostly people thought it made you crazy, sailors and that, because it did nothing to sort your thirst out which made you drink more of it, and then more, and more. I guess that kind of desperation looked a bit crazy if you're stuck in a lifeboat with someone who can't stop. Can't help themselves. But Genna didn't drink it all the time. And it's just a myth anyway, like I said. I just want to mention it so you know what happened wasn't Genna's fault. She didn't *make* herself crazy.

"GOT YOURSELF A stalker," Tommy said at the next gig. We were coming in with the gear and there she was, leaning against the bar, chasing ice cubes around and around with a straw. She was wearing a short dress that was all laces and buckles and promises.

"What can I say? They always want more."

The gig was on the Isle of Wight again, which was a right fucking hassle with the crossing but some pub was paying us well to bring the summer in. It was a late afternoon, early evening thing, still quite light, the bar only half full. Or half empty. Whatever.

"You gonna poke that again?" Vince asked.

"Maybe." I should have said no, but the way she looked tonight…

"Well shove her my way if you don't, I'll give her a go. I'd love to get a bit of that slit."

See? Such a way with words.

Genna was looking into her glass, stirring her whirlpool. Fuck it, I thought, and went over. "Not thirsty?"

I get so thirsty whenever I come here…

I tried not to think about the seawater. And fuck knows what she was thinking because for a moment it was like she didn't even recognise me. Her eyes were far away and I wondered if she was on something, and then I wondered if she was just playing it cooler than me, and then I wasn't wondering anything because she was back and smiling her pearly whites. "Hi!"

"Yeah, hi."

"You taking requests?" she asked.

"Let me guess…"

"'Coastline'."

Which was going to be a problem because this was another covers gig. But I said yes anyway because I'm a fucking idiot sometimes, in case you haven't noticed.

"Maybe we can meet up again after," is what she should have said then, but instead it was *me* saying it.

"Maybe," she said.

Fuck.

The gig was not one of our best. Mainly because my heart just wasn't in it. I just wanted it finished so I could get back to Genna. We went through the usual playlist but really I was just going through the motions.

…the motion of the ocean…

"Okay, this next one is one of ours," I said. "It's called 'Coastline'."

I could feel the others giving me and each other 'what the fuck?' looks but I ignored them and started in with the song so they'd have to go with it. They didn't fucking like it though, and neither did the audience – they wanted something they could sing to, music they could predict. They didn't hate it, they didn't fuck off and leave us, but some of the energy went away and the bar got a bit busier.

I get so thirsty…

Genna loved it. I could even hear her voice at one point, yelling my lyrics back at me when I sang about mermaids riding the waves and the voices that wake us to drown. She whooped and clapped as Hench bashed out a conclusion that was all storm and rocks, cymbals crashing and fading into a shimmering sound of receding waves. Before I could say or do anything else, Tommy took us into 'Going Under' which made a pretty smooth transition actually, the clever prick, and we got our audience back because they weren't really our fans anyway they were Evanescence fans or whatever and what the fuck did I care?

"The hell?" Tommy said when we finished.

"What?"

"Remember that chat we had? About girls not fucking up the group? You know, after Sally?"

Sally was a gorgeous band aid until she got pregnant and ruined it all. She lives up north now. Not sure if she kept the kid.

"I remember."

"Good, because you said most of it."

I nearly told the self-righteous prick about Kate then. That I'd fucked her once and how there's been tension between us ever since. Instead I went with, "She's hardly fucking up the group. I gave her one song."

"Yeah, and it fucking threw us. Vince came in late and–"

"Hey," said Vince, "It wasn't my fault, I–"

"Yeah, I know," said Tommy, "it was this dick's fault."

"Hey, Tommy?"

"What?"

"Fuck off."

And, surprise surprise, he did. He flicked both hands at me dramatically, the diva, but he went.

"Wow," I said, "If I'd known it'd be that easy…"

Vince only shook his head. "Mate, you were a bit of a cunt."

"Whatever."

Genna joined me at the bar. I tried to remember how she looked in the water with her underwear all see-through and wanking me off but all I kept seeing was her drinking seawater with my come in it and I wasn't thirsty anymore.

She must have picked up on that, or maybe she could just tell that I was pissed about something, because she came straight out with, "Back to mine then?"

I looked over to where Hench and Vince were packing up. Tommy wasn't around. He was probably outside, calling Kate on the mainland, bitching about me. She hadn't come tonight – too much hassle – and I was wishing I'd stayed behind as well.

"I live here," Genna said, "Just up the road."

"Okay, cool. Let's go."

Up the road was right. Her place was at the top of a steep hill with a view over the sea to Portsmouth. We barely spoke, and when we did it was just small talk stuff, the kind you have when there's something else unsaid underneath it all. Mostly it was sexual tension, but for me there was a riptide underneath of band shit and concern for Genna's mental stability and all that. But fuck it, any hole's a goal, right?

"Mum? You still up?"

I couldn't fucking believe it.

"You live with your mum?"

"In here, honey."

And so I was led into the front room were a skinny woman in a tatty dressing gown sat watching TV. She looked at me, looked longer at the guitar case in my hands, then looked at Genna.

"This is Josh."

"Hi," I said. Then, after an awkward pause, "Look, Genna—"

"You play guitar, Josh?"

"Er, yeah."

"Any good?"

I looked at Genna to end this but she just smiled at me. "He's great, Mum."

Her mother nodded, "Of course he is," and muted the television.

Here we go…

"What else do you do, Josh?"

"He's in a band, Mum. Breaking Wave. They're really good."

Genna's mother nodded. "I'm sure, honey."

"Josh writes the songs. His lyrics are amazing."

If I had to pick a moment that marked the start of it all, for me, I think it might have been right then. She'd called the band Breaking Wave and never mind what the fuck everybody else called it. And she liked my songs.

"We're going up to my room, okay?"

I could see in the way Genna's mum smiled and said, "Okay," that this was a woman eager to keep her daughter happy. Later I'd realise it was more a case of not wanting her upset, which is a slightly different thing. "I'll bring you both a cup of tea."

"That's okay Mrs—"

"Miss. Do you take sugar, Josh?"

"No, thank you."

"He's sweet enough, Mum."

Genna was already dragging me up the stairs after her and as much as I wanted to leave I was still grateful. I tried not to knock the framed photos with my guitar on the way up. They were all Genna, all pre-goth smiles and all at the seaside. Every single picture. In one of them she wore seaweed like a wig, buried to the waist in sand shaped like a fish tail.

"This is me."

She opened her door and, holy fuck… there were mermaids *everywhere*.

"This one's Waterhouse," Genna said, dancing in and pointing to one of the many posters. Women with fishtails rising from the water in graceful arcs or sitting on rocks to comb their hair, play a tiny harp. "And this one is Leighton. It's called 'The Fisherman and the Syren'." She shrugged. "Slightly different but they get mixed up all the time and anyway, I like it."

There was a picture beside her mirror I recognised.

"That's from the film *Splash*," she said. "You know, with Tom Hanks?"

"Doesn't look like Tom Hanks," I said, and Genna laughed but I stopped looking just in case. Girls get jealous easy, even of pictures. I looked around her room some more.

There were ornaments and statuettes everywhere, even a mermaid lamp. A scattering of shells decorated every surface too, open mussels and clams and even the large spike-edged bulge of one of those that lets you hear the sea, a conch or whatever. She saw me looking and said, "My telephone to the ocean," and picked it up. She put it to my ear. "Listen. What do you hear?" She waited with what I thought was obvious expectation but now I think it was hope.

What I heard was the blood in my ear hushed back at me, but I said, "The sea." She seemed disappointed, maybe at my lack of enthusiasm, and put it back on the table next to a fishbowl where a yellow fish swam circles around a sparkly mermaid spewing bubbles. Above it was a poster that matched her bedspread.

"That one's Disney," she said.

The Little fucking Mermaid.

"How old are you, Genna?"

She laughed but I was serious, and seriously worried.

"Nineteen."

Thank fuck.

"I know, too old."

Better than too young.

I leant my guitar against the wardrobe.

"Look," she said, showing me a video case of the same film. A fucking *video* case; who watched those anymore? "See the difference?"

I looked. All I saw was the same cartoon redhead with clamshells on her tits. And the same yellow fish like the one in her bedside bowl.

"Look at the castle," Genna said. "At the towers. Look."

"Is that…"

"Yeah, a huge golden penis!"

"Shit, it really is."

"Subversive, huh? Some joker at Disney having a laugh. It's only on the video cover though." She threw it onto the bed and followed it. Looking at the face printed beside her on the quilt, her reflection in a pool of bedding, she said, "The original Little Mermaid dies, you know."

"What?"

She nodded. "Yeah, she dies. The prince doesn't love her as much as she loves him and she dies. Turns into sea foam."

"Really?"

"Yeah."

"Well I can see why they'd change that for the cartoon." I didn't like this conversation at all. There seemed to be a threat in it somewhere. "What is it with you and mermaids?"

Genna shrugged. "I'm just mental."

"No you're not."

I tried to tell myself lots of people obsessed about something. Shit, Hench's room was entirely football players, but then he was gay. Probably.

"Some people think mermaids are real," she said. "I mean, there's so much ocean out there we haven't explored properly, so *maybe...*"

I only gave her "Mm."

"Some people think we evolved from mermaids," she said. She made little speech marks with her fingers and added, "Aquatic ape theory."

"Aquatic ape theory," I said. "Okay."

"It's why we don't have much body hair compared to other animals. And more fat."

I remembered what she looked like nearly naked and said, "Now you *are* being mental. There's no fat on you at all."

It was meant to be a compliment but she ignored it. Might've even looked a bit hurt, which was weird.

"Plus our noses stick out," she said, recovering, "nostrils pointing down so we can bob underwater without air getting in." She demonstrated with a ducking motion.

I get so thirsty whenever I come here...

Then she turned profile. "Streamlined for swimming, see? It's why our fingers wrinkle in the bath, too. Improves our grip on rocks and for catching fish, from when we lived more in the water." Then she laughed and said, "And people think *I'm* crazy."

"Even Darwin thought a fish climbed out of the water one day," I said, going to where she sat on the bed. Standing, I was in the perfect position for a blowjob.

"Exactly!" She reached up, but only to take my hands, guiding me down beside her. "In the old days, mermaids used to be in the sea life encyclopaedias, right there with whales and dolphins. You know, real creatures."

"I love these tattoos," I said. I was trying to change the subject, and it was a good excuse to raise the skirt of her dress. I stroked the lines of seaweed on her thighs. She made a noise that was either acknowledgment or encouragement so I carried on.

So did she.

"There was this mermaid who fell in love with a man," she said softly, letting me continue what I was doing. I could tell she was liking it from her breathing. "She gave him precious gifts."

"What precious gifts?"

But I thought, *yes.* Sex. Obviously. This was just her way of leading up to it.

"Trinkets," she said. "Jewels. Pearls, probably. When mermaids cry, they cry pearls."

I looked at how the corset part of her dress squashed her tits up and thought, pearl necklace, yeah. Definitely.

"She kept him in her cave."

Definitely sex.

I could feel her knickers now and was reassured at how damp they were. "Sounds terrible." I said, and moved closer.

I rubbed between her thighs and she told me all about mermaids and selkies and sirens, or tried to; eventually she just groaned and sighed instead and things were looking good for a fuck, *really* fucking good. At *last.*

So of course that was when her mum came in with the tea.

*   *   *

KATE CAME INTO the hall having heard me slam the door.

"Not like you to go back for seconds," she said. "She must be a great shag."

I didn't have a fucking clue, but I said, "Best ever."

"Well I hope you're fucking her in every hole because you've pissed off pretty much everyone."

"Where are they?"

"They went back to Vince's. You know, without you. Because you didn't show up at the ferry."

Vince was the only one in the band who didn't live with us. Kate didn't live with us either but it fucking felt like it. She was always there, even when Tommy wasn't.

"What's so special about this one?"

I ignored her, stomping up the stairs like some frustrated blue-balled teenager. She called up after me. "Got a soft spot for nutjobs?"

"Nothing soft about it."

Kate followed me.

"She doesn't seem your type."

"How's that?"

She smiled. "Well, she's not inflatable for starters."

"Funny." I put my guitar down and cleared my bed of clothes.

"She must fake a good orgasm."

"I've heard plenty of those from Tommy's room."

"I don't fake *all* of them." She smiled again, trying to be mischievous or some shit.

"Not you," I said. "Tommy."

Her smile slipped a little at that. I think because she couldn't tell if I was joking.

"I don't fake *any* orgasms, actually," she said. "Not with *anyone*."

"No, you fake entire relationships."

"Twat."

Finally she left me alone. I shut the door behind her and flopped down next to my guitar. Checked my phone again but still had nothing. Thought about calling. Thought about texting. Didn't do either. I just lay there, thinking of Genna, not even wanking. It was weird.

I was still laying there thinking when the others came home. I heard some laughter and soon people were coming up to bed themselves.

"G'night Josh," Kate called through the door. Tommy tried to shush her, but he was drunk and laughing. She added, "We'll try to keep the noise down."

She didn't. And I managed to have a wank after all.

THE NEXT DAY I got a text from Genna telling me her mum was out and I should come over. There was even a little kiss as well. It was a bit of a mission, getting back over to the Isle of Wight on a Sunday, but the kiss was promising so I text back to say I was on my way.

It wasn't true, though. Her text. Quite the opposite, in fact. Just a trick to get me over.

"It was me who text you," Genna's mum said as soon as she opened the door. I've often wondered how different things would have been if I'd just gone home. But she said there were things I needed to know so I stayed.

She put the kettle on and though neither of us mentioned it I knew we were both thinking about the cup of tea last night. I'd been a knickers slide-aside away from getting laid, so there's another moment to think about, another 'what if?'. What if she'd taken a bit longer with the tea? I could have fucked Genna and *all this mermaid nonsense* would have been sorted.

But I'm telling it out of order. Hang on.

"Sugar?"

I opened my mouth to answer, but she said, "Oh, no, you're sweet enough, isn't that right?"

Yeah, she had my number.

"Mrs–"

"*Miss*. McVeagh."

"Right. Miss McVeagh, I dunno what you–"

"Why don't you let me go first, Josh. See what you want to say when I'm done."

I took my tea from her and put it down quickly before I could burn my fingers too much on the thin china. "Okay."

"Genna's adopted, did she tell you that?"

I shook my head. "No."

"She went through a few foster parents first, and then me and my husband adopted her."

"Your husband?"

"Gone. Not important."

She thought about that for a moment then said, "Well, maybe it is important. Her real daddy left when she was little. Then her mum tried to kill herself and Genna too."

What the fuck?

"Yeah."

I hadn't said it aloud, but it must have showed.

"She walked into the sea carrying baby Genna in her arms. God knows how such a wee thing survived, but she did."

I didn't know what to say, or even if I was supposed to say anything, so I tried my tea. It was still ridiculously hot but I forced myself.

"One of her early foster parents made up some stuff about mermaids and it stuck." She smiled but it wasn't a nice one. If she hadn't already said, I'd have known then that Genna was adopted. "Mermaids took Genna's parents, apparently. And now Genna wants to be one."

"A mermaid."

Miss McVeagh had no trouble with her tea. She took a scalding swallow. "They probably thought they were helping, making up a story, telling Genna she was too young at the time to change. Become a mermaid."

"That had to be tough."

She looked at me over the top of her tea, through the steam, then put the cup down again.

"Sometimes she says she hears her mother, her real mother, singing from the taps," she said. "And from the sink. The drains. Sometimes she speaks to her on the sea-phone."

"The–"

"Sea-phone. The shell in her room, the big one. So you see, Josh, she's a troubled girl. And she's heard all these other mermaid stories and they're all about love and they've become mixed in with each other so now she thinks to find love she needs to be a mermaid. Or if she finds love she'll become a mermaid. Something like that. You can't understand what it's like, Josh."

I thought I did, actually. Wanting something you couldn't have.

"She loves you, you know."

"Who?"

"She's been going to your gigs, up and down the coast. Plus I found this in her room." She put Genna's hip flask on the table. "She's done this before."

"She doesn't have a drinking problem, Miss McVeagh. She just sneaks that into the pubs. Because it's cheaper."

"Open it."

I did.

"Taste it."

I only had to smell it.

"Seawater. She thinks if she drinks enough of it..." she shrugged. "I don't know. She started doing it, off and on, after her first period."

Fucking hell.

"Miss–"

"Just wait, Josh. I'm nearly done. I know you men are squeamish about these things but that was when she... got worse. She thought her period meant it was too late, that the bleeding meant she was permanently split down there–"

"I better–"

"She thought it meant her legs were permanent. She was a confused girl. She still is."

"I'll stop seeing her. If that's what you want."

It was what I wanted. I didn't need all this shit.

"Well, that's up to you. She's gone to yours though."

"*What?*"

"We had an argument, just before I text you."

I could guess what about.

Miss McVeagh followed me to the door.

"Look after her, Josh. Just for tonight. Let her stay over. She likes you, you could have sex with her and stop all this mermaid nonsense, mermaids are virgins you see. Or you could break her heart. Christ, you could even do both if it sorts her out."

I wasn't sure Genna got all her crazy from her birth mother.

I didn't say goodbye.

I didn't exactly hurry home, either.

"ABOUT FUCKING TIME," was how Hench greeted me as I let myself in.

"Genna here?"

"Yeah, Genna's here." He pointed at the downstairs bathroom. "She's been here a couple of hours. Where have *you* been?"

"She have bags with her?"

"Carrier bags, yeah. Some shopping. And a backpack. Why?"

I knocked on the bathroom door. "Genna? You in there?"

"Why'd you ask about bags, man? Is she moving in or something?"

"Genna?"

I could hear she was in there. She was crying, but trying to do it quietly. And I could hear the quiet swishes and splashes of her movement in the bathwater.

"She's been in there pretty much the whole time," Hench said.

"You the only one in?"

Hench nodded.

"Genna, I'm going to come in if you don't answer me."

"She's been in there for nearly two hours," Hench said.

"Yeah, okay, you've said. Fuck off."

"Hey, I'm just saying—"

"And I'm just saying she won't let me in if you're stood out here with me. Go for a walk or something."

Hench held up his hands like I was overreacting but he did as he was told. I'd been an asshole, I knew that, but I could fix that later. Or not.

"Genna?"

Still nothing but quiet sniffling and splashing.

We've got a shitty lock on our bathroom door, one of those you can open from the outside with a screwdriver or piece of cutlery. I've got guitarist's fingernails though, which were enough.

There was towel on the floor and it caught under the door so that it wouldn't open all the way at first, but even open just a little bit I was hit by the smell.

"Christ!"

It was fish. A really fucking strong stink of fish. I remember thinking, shit, she really does need a bath and then I had the door all the way open and I saw what was going on.

"Fuck, Genna, what the *fuck*?"

I shut the door behind me immediately and locked it again in case anyone else came home, even though it trapped me in with the smell.

Genna was sitting in the bath, her makeup running down her face. She looked like she was crying oil. She was naked, her glorious tits right there for me to see, but I barely noticed right then because I was looking in the bath. It was full of fish. Dead ones, floating, some of them spilling their guts in the water. She had one in her hands. I know fuck all about fish so I can only tell you they were pretty big and a silvery dark colour. A shit load of their scales glittered on the surface of the water.

"What's going on, sweetheart?"

Sweetheart?

She still hadn't said anything or reacted in any way to suggest she knew I was there. She just stuck her fingers into the fish's belly and opened it up with her nails. Then she rubbed the split fish up and down her legs.

"It's not working," she said. She swapped legs and rubbed the fish up her body again as if it was soap. "It's not *fuck*ing *work*ing." Her voice hitched for breath between words. Christ knows how long she'd been crying, but she sounded exhausted by it.

She dropped one fish and swilled around the scales and bodies for another one, a fresh one. There must have been two, three dozen of the fuckers in there with her, floating around. Squashed up against the bathtub beneath her foot, one of them had folded around her toes like some novelty slipper. Another seemed to nuzzle between her thighs and somehow I managed to notice she was shaved bare down there. That nuzzling fish was the one she took hold of next, dragging her nails under it, splitting it open, shining her legs with its flattened body and everything that glistened and emptied from inside.

"Genna, no. Stop it, Genna."

I went to my knees at the side of the tub and took the fish from her hands. She let me do it. I threw it back in the water and then took her arms to pull her hands away from her face. She was proper sobbing now and covering her face as if she didn't want me to see. Like I hadn't seen enough already.

"Genna, come on." I pulled at her wrists and she let me do that too. She'd probably let me do anything, state she was in.

…have sex with her and stop all this mermaid nonsense…

"Genna, sweetheart, look at me."

Her eyes were black circles with lines running down her face, and her cheeks sparkled with fish scales where she'd put her hands, iridescent fantails of silver rising up from her cheekbones and spread around her eyes like that glitter shit some girls wear.

"It's okay," I said, even though it definitely fucking wasn't okay. The girl was proper damaged. But still.

"It's not *working*," she said again, quietly this time, imploring me like I could somehow fix it. "It's supposed to make me… make me…" But her sobs were so violent she couldn't get the words out.

"I know, I know," I said, partly so she could stop trying. Partly because I really didn't want to hear it. That would be like admitting how fucked up she was, though it was already obvious.

"You know what I read the other day?" I said, trying to calm her down. "About mermaids? I read about them and apparently, if you drink the seawater from a drowned man's lungs then you can breathe underwater like they do."

I didn't know what the fuck I was saying. I was just trying to stop her from crying, get her out of the bath so that I could tidy the whole mess up before the others came home.

"I mean, it's not quite a mermaid, but it's a start, yeah?"

And okay, part of me was just trying to make her happy. Fucking sue me. I wanted to give her something to cling to.

She wiped her eyes but only managed to spread more makeup and scales across her face. "Where did you read that?"

"I dunno. Maybe I didn't read it, maybe it was on TV. Maybe it was on that channel with the documentaries, yeah? Anyway, it said in the old days people drank the water from a drowned man's lung so they could live with the mermaids. You know, because they were in love with them? They drank it and they could breathe underwater. I think for a year?"

I was making this shit up as I went. And it got worse.

"I know a guy who works in the hospital," I told her. "Next time they get a drowned person in, I'll get him to keep the water if you want."

She sniffed, and she must have got a right fucking chestful of that fish stink but she didn't seem to care. She wiped her nose.

"Does it have to be a man?" she asked.

"What?"

"You said a drowned man. Does it have to be a man?"

"I don't think it matters."

She tilted her head and looked at me like I was the one being crazy and said, "It's magic, *everything* matters. Every detail."

"Well just to be safe we'll only use one that comes from a man, okay?"

She sniffed again, and nodded, and I didn't care how fucking doolally that made her as long as she was calming down.

"Do you have to drink it from the lung?"

"What? No."

"You said they drink water from a drowned man's lung. Do you mean the water comes from the lung or it has to actually be drunk from the lung?"

"No, just the water."

The best smile she ever gave me was right then. It was so grateful it almost hurt to see, and I've wondered about a billion times since if she knew I was full of shit but just smiled anyway.

She reached for the towel. I handed it to her. She wiped her face and saw the makeup stains and scale-shimmer on the towel. "Sorry."

"That's okay."

She stood up and the water rinsed off of her, leaving the skin of her lower body silver-shiny with scales. If it wasn't for all the dead fish bobbing in the water, and the fucking awful smell, it would have been pretty sexy, in a weird kinda way. Exotic or erotic or something. And she did have the most amazing body. I stood up with her, aware of where my head would be if I didn't, but she quickly wrapped the towel around her waist anyway. The bottom of the towel fell into the water but what the hell did that matter at this point? I offered her my hand to help her step out of the bath.

"Thank you," she said.

"That's okay."

I kept saying it, like I could make it true.

"I had an argument with my mum."

"I know. That's okay."

That's okay, that's okay, that's okay.

"I'll get dressed."

"No rush."

I meant it as in take your time, no hurry, stay calm, all of that, but she raised her eyebrow at me and said, "Oh, really?" She glanced down at her half naked body and back at me. "Do you like what you see?"

That was a pretty fucking complicated question, but I looked. She was practically begging me to. She stepped closer and, yeah, her tits felt as good as they looked. She started undoing my jeans.

"Genna…"

"To say thank you."

I swallowed whatever I was going to say next because she knelt and then I was in her mouth. I meant to stop her but then I didn't want to and even though the room stank and she was fucking crazy I sat down on the toilet seat to get more comfortable and she curled up at my feet, playing her mouth over me. Thinking about it now, she was probably fantasising about being a mermaid, but that was okay because with the glittering scales on her skin and the way the wet towel was wrapped around her legs, fanned out at the bottom to hide her feet like a tail… Well, I was thinking about mermaids too. Until all I could think about was whether to come in her mouth or on her tits and then I didn't care about mermaids anymore.

GENNA SHOWERED IN the upstairs bathroom while I cleaned the one downstairs. By the time I was done she was tucked up in my bed, all fresh and clean, her hair still wet. She'd wrapped the quilt around herself and was looking at a notepad I keep on the bedside table.

"Are these new songs?"

Normally I'm sensitive as fuck about that kind of thing. "Eventually," I said. She leafed back through the pad as I tidied the room a bit, though she'd already seen what a shithole it was.

"I like this one."

She quoted some lines about dark quiet seas. Of course she liked that one. She turned the pages back, back, time travelling into my past through my lyrics.

"'Coastline'," she said.

"Yeah."

"I love 'Coastline'."

"I know." I sat on the edge of the bed. "It's not all mine. I nicked some from a poem." I'd never admitted that before.

"You read poetry?"

Only on my phone, so nobody sees. I didn't say that, though. I just shrugged, no big deal, and recited lines about mermaids combing their hair, sea-girls wreathed in seaweed, human voices. Drowning.

"What poem?"

"T.S. Eliot. A poem about a guy too scared to live his life properly."

"I like this bit best," she said, and read from the notepad. And it was *my* bit. Lines about beaches and cliffs and the to and fro of tides not belonging. She preferred *my* lines.

I don't know what she saw in my face, but she smiled and flipped the notepad to its most recent page before handing it back. She'd drawn a cartoon, a caricature with elements of Disney, but he had the same hair, the same too-big smile I used when trying to be charming, and a guitar. The guitar was strung with seaweed.

"Ha! I love it!"

In the other hand I held what I'd assumed was a bouquet of flowers at first but turned out to be a bunch of spiky fish bones, all spines and lines and wilting half-circle heads with crosses for eyes.

Genna moved over in the bed. "Come on," she said.

I turned the covers back and saw she was wearing pyjamas, proper trouser ones with long sleeves too, and found I didn't mind. In fact, there was something pretty intimate about seeing her that way that I liked. I took off my jeans and climbed in beside her in my shorts and t-shirt.

It was the best night of my life. We didn't even do anything. We just talked. Can you believe that? True even if you don't. She told me some of what her mother, her foster mother or whatever, had told me but quickly shifted the focus to my songs instead of going into detail. It was easy to do because of that dark quiet seas bit, "The whispered hush of a dark quiet tide." She snuggled into my shoulder and draped one of her legs over mine, her arm over my chest; exactly the sort of position I usually hated. But I didn't shrug her away. "I'm looking for someone to share the darkness with too," she said.

We talked all night, it felt like. A lot of it was about my songs. Genna understood them. She fucking understood what I was talking about. Understood *me*.

"You know, Eric Clapton – or just Eric, if you're Tommy – he once said the blues were easy to play but difficult to feel." I looked at Genna to see if she was following.

"A white boy making his excuses," she said, and I laughed. I mean, she was exactly right. But it wasn't my point.

"Yeah," I said. "But I mean, Hench, Vince, Tommy; they can play it, and they sing the lines okay, but they don't feel it properly. They don't get it."

"I do."

She did. She even managed to explain 'Rye-Catcher' and I realised I did know what I was doing when I didn't get swept up in all the bullshit. Genna made it make sense.

"But who's Crossfire Girl?"

"Hmm?"

I was drifting off by then, lulled to near-sleep by her voice.

"Crossfire Girl. The one 'caught in the middle and loving it', who's she?"

"I dunno. Nobody." I stroked her hair and kissed the top of her head. Before she could ask anything else I said, "You know, I read up on mermaids."

"Yeah, you said. Was that because of me?"

"Yeah."

"That's nice."

"I read about them peeling their skin off and–"

"That's selkies." She stirred, raised herself to look at me. "They're not the same thing."

"Oh. Okay. Anyway, I'm beginning to feel a bit like that with all this stuff about my songs."

I was joking, but it was true, too.

Genna laughed sleepily and settled back into me. "Okay. Yeah, sorry. I'll stop analysing you." She kissed my shoulder. "Anyway, it's me who needs analysing. I'm the one who's mental."

"Everybody wants to be something else," I said. "Look at me. How are you any different to me or the band, pretending we'll make it big one day?"

She rose up again, this time to kiss me on the mouth. To look into my eyes. "*You'll* make it," she said. "*You'll* be okay."

Somehow I'd made it all about me again when I should have been talking about her. I should have been helping Genna.

She lay down again, nuzzled in close, and put her hand between my legs. Not to do anything, just to hold me. "You taste salty," she said. "It's nice."

Maybe she meant the kiss, maybe she meant earlier, I dunno. We were falling asleep by then anyway.

"We should go to that aquarium," I murmured. "The one in Brighton."

"Mmm."

We fell asleep entwined together and in the night, when we stirred to separate, I didn't even try to grab her tits or her ass or anything. We just held hands and went back to sleep.

SOME PEOPLE SAY drowning is the most peaceful way to die. That it's like falling asleep. I'm not so sure about that. Imagine that first breath you take, how it must feel to have water rushing into a space where air used to go. Imagine how heavy it must make your lungs. How cold it is, cold from the inside out.

Apparently your body won't let you do it until you're close to unconsciousness. You hold your breath right up until you're physically unable to hold it anymore. By that point I reckon your body and brain is thinking, fuck it, we'll die if we don't breathe *something*, and then gives water a try. It gets dark, too, apparently. The lack of oxygen makes everything dim. Not that I imagine there's an awful lot to see underwater anyway. A curious fish, maybe. Unless Genna was right about the dead haunting the cold water. Maybe they watch it happen before taking you with them in the ebbing tide.

Some people *can't* drown. There's this thing that happens in the throat like an automatic switch or something, closes it off, stops the water coming in. They still die, they suffocate, but it's purely from a lack of oxygen, not because their lungs have filled up with water.

They both sound pretty fucking horrible to me.

WE TRIED THE dead man's lungs thing. I filled an old Coke bottle with water, stirred a shit load of salt in there, and added a bit of red colouring because I'd read that the struggle to breathe when you're drowning bursts blood vessels or something. Then I remembered her hip flask, changed my mind and tipped it. She'd know it wasn't seawater. So I went to the beach and bottled the real thing, adding the colour again. It was a bit pink, but it would do. It was probably wrong, feeding into her delusion or whatever I was doing, but I didn't want to fuck her just to *stop this mermaid nonsense*. I wanted to do something for her and, as fucked up as it was, this was the best I could think of.

She believed me when I told her what it was supposed to be. We were on Ryde Beach. I'd gone to the Isle of Wight instead of band practice because, you know, fuck that lot. They'd given me shit about the bathroom, even when I tried to explain. Plus Genna was trying to fix things with her mother or whatever so it was good to stay close. "Bit soon to be moving in anyway," she said, and smiled.

"Yeah."

But then, fuck knows why, I gave her my key.

"You can come over whenever you need to," I said. "You know. Just to crash or whatever."

Genna looked at it but didn't take it.

"It's okay," I said. "There's a spare behind the drainpipe I can use."

She took the key and smiled and I knew I'd done the right thing. That smile. Jesus, that smile. She put the key in her purse. "It doesn't freak you out?"

It did a bit, but then I saw she was pointing at the Coke bottle between us on the sand.

"I've seen you wiping dead fish up your legs," I said. "This is fine."

She laughed. "You should've seen the time I tried to sew them together."

"*What?*"

She took the bottle and twisted off the lid, looked inside. "I was eleven, just started my period." She inhaled from the bottle like it was fine wine. "Anyway, I thought if I sewed my legs together then the skin would heal over into a tail. I managed both thighs and was struggling with my knees when my foster mother found me." Genna looked at me. "Lucky, really, considering what I would have sewn up next." She smiled, but not a real one. "So she found me and grabbed my hand to stop me and that was the only time it actually hurt. Only place I needed stitches was where she tore the fishhook from my skin."

"*Fishhook?*"

"Yeah."

She was sitting cross-legged on the sand but fidgeted to hike up the skirt of her dress. I noticed she was wearing lacy green knickers. She showed me a jagged scar at the side of her kneecap.

"I was using fishing line and one of Peter's hooks," she said. "Not my real dad, but you know. I liked him. He liked me too, I thought." She shrugged, covering herself up again, and started swilling the bottle in circular motion, stirring a whirlpool of its contents. I wondered if she could tell it was only food colouring. "Anyway," she said, looking at me. "Let's see if this works."

I had the feeling she meant more than the crap in the Coke bottle.

"Be careful," I said, maintaining eye contact. "Too much can make you crazy."

"Yeah. I've heard that."

She downed it in one.

"Feel different?"

She kissed me full on the mouth. I could taste the salt on her lips. Before we could get any more passionate, though, she pulled away and stood up – "Let's find out!" – and ran away from me towards the sea.

"Genna!"

Without even taking off her clothes she splashed into the surf, leaping over what waves there were and laughing like a child. It really wasn't the weather for it, but when the water was deep enough she arched into a dive and was gone.

"Genna!"

I followed as far as the wet sand, dancing back from each wave that slid up the beach, looking out to sea for her to reappear.

She didn't.

"Fuck."

I stepped on the heels of my shoes, pulled them off, and was just grabbing for the buttons on my shirt when she came up again. She was ridiculously far out, a much faster swimmer than I could ever be, faster than I imagined possible outside of the Olympics, and she turned to wave at me. I waved back but she had already dipped back under.

She was gone for so long that I readied myself to undress again, thinking *not waving, drowning*, but then she rose up from the shallows nearby, sweeping her wet hair back from her face and emerging from the sea like some gorgeous Bond girl. Only, you know, fully dressed. She was still gorgeous. Her dress clung to her and the straps had fallen down to show a lot more cleavage than intended. With her legs still hidden in the water, and the skirts flowing around her on the surface of the water, it was easy to see her as the mermaid she wanted to be. She was smiling and she was absolutely beautiful. I went to her, not caring about how the sea came in and filled my shoes, soaked my socks, the cuffs of my jeans.

"It was brilliant!" she called, wading to shore. She looked over her shoulder at all that ocean behind and turned a little to face it, her hair hanging straight down her back. She said something I didn't hear and then she was facing me again, and smiling, and coming towards me.

As soon as she was close enough I gathered her into my arms. I had no jacket for her but I held her close and shivering against me. She hadn't been cold that night at the pier but I didn't think about that then. I think about it now, though, and I reckon she made a choice that day that really affected her. Let something go. We staggered back up the beach together.

"I saw them," she said. "I saw their faces in the water."

"Who?"

"In the cold water," she said. "You know, the really cold water? I saw them."

"You're freezing," I said, because I couldn't think of anything else.

"No wonder they lure people in. They're lonely, swimming with just the dead for company." She looked at me and laughed with delight. "I saw them!"

"Yeah," I said. What the hell else was I meant to say? "Yeah. That happens sometimes. I didn't want to tell you about it in case it didn't work." But I had the strangest feeling she was lying. I mean, for my sake or something.

"It was weird. I couldn't breathe, though, not yet. I tried, but it still went down like water instead of air."

"Maybe it takes time."

"Yeah, maybe. I *could* hold my breath for longer."

"See?" I squeezed her hard so she knew I was hugging her as well as holding her. "It's working."

She kissed me again, this time with more passion than simply thanks.

"Let's get you out of these wet clothes," I said. I waggled my eyebrows.

"I love you, Josh."

You might not believe this bit, but right then, behind her, I saw someone else standing in the sea looking our way. The sky was grey, and breezy, and it was beginning to spit with rain, but someone was out there in the water. They were far away, but I could see enough to know they were watching. I wanted to tell Genna but I couldn't get the words out, couldn't get any words out. I just opened and closed my mouth, feeling way in over my head with this.

"Come on, let's go back to mine," Genna said. "Mum's not in today."

The woman in the sea – I'm pretty sure it was a woman – waved the same way Genna had when she was out there and then a distant wave rolling in to shore swallowed her up and she was gone.

WE WENT STRAIGHT to her bedroom but I was left there to wait while she dried herself in the bathroom. I was a little wet myself but nothing major and anyway, I figured it would all be coming off in a minute.

I looked around her room again. Mermaids here, mermaids there. I found a picture of her and Miss McVeagh and a man I assumed to be Peter. He could only have looked more like a fisherman if he'd been holding a fish to the camera; thick woollen jumper, beard, fishing rod leaning against the pier rail behind him. He had both his arms around Genna from behind, both of them grinning, even Miss McVeagh managing a tight smile.

I picked up the conch and said, "Hello," quietly to the shush I heard there. I said, "Don't worry, I'll look after her." Then I felt like an idiot and put it down, which was just as well because Genna came back.

She was wearing a short dressing gown and rubbing her hair dry in a towel decorated with starfish.

"I used to feel a lot like that shell," she said, and I realised she must have seen me putting it down. I hoped she hadn't heard me speaking into it. Or, considering what I'd said, maybe I hoped she did. I dunno, this was all new to me.

"Filled with the sea?" I said.

"Empty. Haunted by a sea that only said ssh, ssh, and slipped away from me." She laughed. "Wow, melodramatic, huh?"

"Actually, I thought I might steal it for a song."

She tilted her head and sort of half smiled, half looked sad. "Oh Josh," she said. "I'm so lucky I've got you now."

"I dunno about that."

And right then it was me who was lucky, very lucky, because she came to me and we kissed and her dressing gown fell open and we sat on the bed, lay on the bed, me, Genna, and a redhead mermaid thrusting up over a rock, and after a while of kissing and touching Genna whispered, again, "I love you, Josh."

…you could have sex with her and stop all this mermaid nonsense…

…you could break her heart…

The front door banged closed. "Genna?"

"No," I muttered, slumping against Genna. "Please, no."

"Genna? Are you home?"

Genna fumbled back into her dressing gown and tied it shut. "Hang on."

I wondered if it would matter, if her mum would just pimp her out like she tried before, but then there was another voice on the stairs, a male voice, "Guess who," and I didn't need Genna to tell me.

"Daddy!"

She ran into him just as he appeared in the doorway and he swept her into a fierce hug. It wasn't daddy, not really, it was Peter. Same jumper and everything. And as fierce as the hug was, it didn't stop him looking past her shoulder at me on the bed. My shirt was unbuttoned more than I'd usually wear it, but it was still on. I picked up the starfish towel as casually as I could and held it in my lap to hide my hard-on, though it was wilting pretty damn quick.

"This is Josh," said Genna, bright and perky.

Peter nodded. I nodded.

"Your mum and I want to talk to you," he said to Genna. "Maybe Josh and I can talk next time."

Genna looked at me and I shrugged. Peter put his arms around her like in the photo.

"Actually," he said, "I can give you a lift to the ferry port."

Genna looked between both of us but I said, "Okay, thanks," before she could say anything.

You wanna know the first thing he said to me in the car? "You're making it worse, Josh." He tried to fix it a bit by saying, "I know you think you're helping," and then he ruined it by adding, "but you're not."

Me, I didn't say anything. Partly I thought he might even be right. Fuck, no, I *knew* he was right. But it didn't seem fair.

"Do you love her, Josh?"

"I…"

To be really blunt about it, how the fuck would I *know*?

Peter nodded. We were at the ferry port by then anyway. "Safe crossing," he said. "Water's a bit choppy."

It didn't look like it to me but I guess he was right because I felt sick the whole way back.

BY THE TIME I got home I was in a foul mood, frustrated with the world and myself and everything that just seemed to get so complicated all on its fucking own. Luckily the house was empty because I was not ready to deal with anyone else's shit right then. And I still had no messages. Nothing. She'd probably never open her legs anyway, I thought, because that would mean she had some.

"Fuck her," I said, pushing my guitar over like some kid having a tantrum. I collapsed onto the bed. "*Fuck* her."

"Who?"

Great. The house *wasn't* empty.

"What are you doing here, Kate?"

She was wrapped in a towel and held another at her hair, head tilted as she rubbed it dry in the doorway. "Oh, hello Kate, how are you?" she said. "I've got to use the shower up here because someone blocked the downstairs bath, didn't they?"

"What are you doing *here*? Where's Tommy? Where's everybody else?"

"Still practising." She shrugged. "Where's your mermaid?"

"Fuck off Kate."

"Come on, Josh. Into bed but not in your head, isn't that the motto? Seriously, what are you doing?"

I didn't have a fucking clue. I thought maybe part of it was feeling sorry for her, and for some reason I said that bit out loud.

"You feel *sorry* for her? Well that's romantic."

"Fuck off, Kate."

"I mean, that's your Valentine's card right there."

"Fuck *off*, Kate."

She threw her towel at me, the one she'd been using on her hair, "Be nice," then combed her hair back with her fingers. She'd dyed it red. Same fucking shade and everything. I couldn't exactly pretend not to notice.

"Jesus, Kate."

I *could* pretend not to notice how combing it back raised her chest in the towel she was wearing. But apparently I couldn't pretend very well.

"What are you looking at?"

"Kate…"

She held up her hands. "Okay, all right." She came in and took the other towel back from me. "How do you fuck a mermaid anyway?"

I stood up quick and pushed her towards the door. Held her waist and walked her backwards out of my room. But she just laughed.

"I suppose she could give you a blowjob," she said, stumbling, catching the other towel before it could fall. "Or you could come on her tits or something." I let her go and grabbed the door to close in her face, fully intending to slam it, but the guitar I'd pushed over was in the way.

Kate sighed. "All right, okay, I'm going."

She dropped both towels.

"But if you ever want a proper fuck again, just let me know."

Do you love her, Josh?

I looked away. At least I did that. But what I saw was the notepad on the bedside table and that ridiculous cartoon version of me, the fake me, all smiles and charm and a bouquet of fish flowers.

…have sex with her and stop all this mermaid nonsense…

When I put my hands on her waist it was to stop her, it really was, but they didn't stay there when she began walking me backwards the same way I'd done to her. By the time we reached the bed I was helping her with my jeans. She sat me down and straddled me.

"Kate—"

But fuck knows what I was going to say. She was already lowering herself onto my lap by then anyway, guiding me inside with one hand. The satisfied groan was both of ours.

"See?" she said. "How good is that?"

"*Kate…*"

She rose up, and then she lowered. "Yeah?"

But I still didn't know what I was going to say.

"Yeah?"

Pretty soon we were both saying it, only it wasn't a question any more.

THERE'S NOT MUCH more to tell. Genna caught us, of course. Kate was laying across my chest afterwards and I was stroking her new hair. Even when she said, "Genna," I only said "yeah" because that's who I was thinking about. So she nudged me.

"What?"

Genna was standing in the doorway. She had her backpack in one hand and my key in the other. "I needed to see you," she said.

I couldn't think of a single word to say. It would've only made things worse anyway, though how things could've been worse I have absolutely no fucking idea, not with Kate clearly naked draped all over me. I pushed her away but all that did was emphasise her nakedness by putting her tits on show. She made no move to cover herself.

"They want to send me away again," Genna said. "To get better." Then, as if realising something important, "You gave me your *key*." She held it up like a prize.

"Genna—"

"Seriously?" Kate said. "Your key?"

That was when Genna ran. She dropped her bag and the key and ran away from what she'd seen. Ran away from me.

"Genna!"

"Just leave her," Kate said.

I pulled on my clothes, fucking it all up as I went.

"You don't need her now," Kate said. With Kate's smile you never know if she's kidding or not and I hesitated. After everything, I still fucking hesitated.

Kate pulled the sheets to her chest as if suddenly modest, despite all we'd just done, and said, "Fuck it," then made a show of looking around the room, "Where are your cigarettes?"

The key lay on one of the damp towels in the doorway. The towel was stained with hair dye but it looked like blood.

"Nice," Kate said, showing me the cartoon version of myself, grinning like a fucking retard, a fist full of fish bones. "Did you do this?"

I ran after Genna.

IN THE LITTLE Mermaid the girl wants to be human, but who'd want that? Her tail splits, every step she takes on her new legs feels like walking on shards of glass, and she loses her tongue too, I think, so basically it *hurts* being human. She changes a lot to try to win this guy and it's really painful for her and then he goes and fucks it all up. So she runs into the sea, only she can't fucking swim now, can she, not with legs, and she drowns. Something like that. I don't remember and I don't feel like checking. Feels right, though. Feels fucked up enough to be right. Don't change who you are just to be with someone or something.

I don't know. It's just a fucking fairy tale. I'm not trying to say it's anything to do with Genna and me. But I do wonder about it a lot. That, and the one she told me about the mermaid with precious gifts. The one where the dickhead gives them to someone else. She takes him away to her cave in the deep dark depths of the sea and keeps him prisoner forever. That one feels pretty fucking spot on.

Genna didn't go to the ferry or the hovercraft. I went to both, and I waited around, but after a while I walked the beach instead, which is what I should have done in the first place. I found her clothes at the South Parade Pier. A neat folded pile on the stones. I half expected to find her skin too, like some fleshy onesie, but the skin thing is selkies, not mermaids. I've held on to her clothes, though. Just in case.

Sometimes when I dream of looking for Genna, I do find a pile of stripped off skin with her clothes. There's sand stuck to the inside where it's red and wet, and it smells of salt and blood, but it's not her skin, it's mine. She didn't want it anymore, and who can blame her? Why the fuck did she even want it in the first place? The music, says the sea. Every breaking wave of the ocean says to me, the music, the music. That's what lured her in. Me, I was just the rock she dashed herself against.

I like to think she lives in some sand-strewn cavern beneath the sea now, and sleeps inside a giant oyster shell in a city where the pavements are made of pearl or something. Somewhere beyond the sea, waiting for me, like in the song. Whereas me, I'm stuck in that cold water she told me about. It surrounds me, now. And what is love if not water for drowning?

You know, once the drowning process starts it doesn't let up, it just gets quicker. Gets worse. Unless you have one of those weird switches that stops it.

Anyway, I stand there, in the dream, hearing my siren songs washing ashore, all of it water for drowning, and it stings my skin because I don't have any. All I am now is raw and sore with brine. And in my mouth, the taste of seawater, as if I'm chasing her madness to follow after. But they're only tears and they don't do anything. If she'd been a selkie they might have called her back but she's not.

I think everybody has one that got away but Genna didn't get away, not really. There's no sand-strewn cave or giant oyster shell for her, no palace of coral. But people will believe anything if it makes them happy. Even if they know it isn't real. When the paper said a girl had been washed up I didn't read it, but I did wonder if the poor girl, whoever she was, made the water colder.

I have a dream sometimes where they keep on washing up, a whole beach full of drowned girls, and Genna steps out from the sea to walk amongst them, wincing with pain. She splits the skin of her chest open with her nails like I saw with the fish in the bath, and she peels back her skin, and I think, thank *fuck*, she *is* a selkie, but she only opens herself enough to reach inside. She wrenches something free and offers it to me dripping but it's not her heart. It's the twin sacks of her lungs, bloated full with the sea, and she offers them to me smiling.

I grope around in the dark for her webbed hand but it's never there.

SHARK! SHARK!

WE'LL BEGIN RIGHT away with the title.

"Shark! Shark!"

We're on a beach in the summer. I could tell you about how beautiful and clean the stretch of sand is, and how the sea is calm and bright and blue beneath a sky that's just the same, but you won't care about that now, not when someone's calling, "Shark!" The cry comes from a blonde woman in a bikini, her hands cupped around her mouth, looking around the crowd. "Shark!"

But it's not what you think. She's a director, one of *two* directors actually, calling for the shark man. The shark man is just some guy, no one for you to worry about. Here he comes, with a big ol' fin on a board, making his way through the crowd of extras. He'll be swimming with that above him in a minute and not only is that the only part he'll play in the film but it's the only part he plays in this story.

That's a lot of onlys, I know. Forget them. Look at the directors instead. They're a husband and wife team. The wife looks Scandinavian but isn't. You've seen her already. She's the blonde in the bikini, of course, making it look good even in her late thirties, body streamlined and supple. Not your typical director attire, perhaps, but this is California (although, for the sake of the film it's Palm Beach, Florida). Anyway, bikini or not, her baseball cap has 'director' printed on it, only without the inverted commas. The husband's the big man with the curled greying hair and the scraggly beard. Nothing neat and Spielbergy for him, oh no. This guy could be a lumberjack. But he's not, he's British, in his forties, and he's a director. His cap says so, just like hers, but he never wears it, just lets it rest on the canvas seat that also has 'director' printed on it (without the inverted commas).

"I want you to swim out to the raft and just circle it a coupla times, 'k?"

The shark man nods at her while looking at her breasts, thinking that because she wears sunglasses she can't see him looking when actually that only works when it's the other way around. He's stupid. He won't go far, not even in movies.

"Jesus," she says as shark man heads for the sea.

Her husband says, "Will I do?"

She swats at his butt, what he would call his arse, because they still have that kind of relationship. Even on set they are very firmly husband and wife.

"Seriously, what is it?" He's looking at her breasts, but that's okay because he's her husband and anyway, they're good breasts.

"Shark guy was doing what you're doing right now."

"Well, they're good breasts."

"Thanks."

"Real, too. And so much in this business isn't."

"You're so deep."

"Deep as the ocean, baby." He flashes her a smile that's bright in his beard and it's the same smile he caught her with all those years ago, although the beard is different now. More grey. She smiles back and he sees this as encouragement, as men trying to be funny often do, and so he continues. "The people in this country of yours aren't used to seeing anything real. Except Coca Cola, of course. That's the real thing. You gotta cut him some slack."

"Can I just cut him?"

"Sorry."

The two of them look out to sea where extras hold their position in the shallows.

"You think if we use that Coke line in the movie it will count as product placement?"

"Can you see him yet?"

The wife has one hand up to shield her eyes from the sun, even though she's wearing sunglasses. The light on the water dazzle-flashes her as it moves with breeze and tide.

"There he is."

"Swimming?"

"Yep. Unless it's a real shark."

The wife, who deserves a name really so let's call her Sheila (although she's not Australian, just like she's not Scandinavian), cups her hands around her mouth and shouts, "Action!"

Bobby, that's her husband, says the same thing into a handheld radio and they are filming, baby. Making movies.

THE FILM BEGAN as a conversation in a bar about *Jaws*. (The film they're making doesn't actually begin that way. It begins with a water-skier discovering a body. She hits it, in fact, and there's a tumbling splash and then she surfaces and it's floating right at her in the wake of the boat and that scene alone will probably get them an R rating but we don't care about that.) The film doesn't begin with a conversation in a bar about *Jaws*, but the *making* of the film begins that way. The idea, which turned into a script, which eventually became casting and all the rest of it, *that* began in a bar with a conversation about *Jaws*.

Glad that's clear.

"Seriously, has there ever been a decent shark movie since?"

"Can there be? I mean, it's kinda difficult to top. Even the man himself couldn't do it, no matter how many times he tried."

"Be fair, he didn't do the sequels."

Her husband supports that statement as a good point by raising his glass and toasting it. He's drinking something that's red and orange and yellow, a sunset in a glass, and it has some fruit stuck on the rim. Little details like that are important. Not to the story so much, but the general sense of atmosphere. Exotic, sunny, fun. You're meant to like this guy, this couple, and if you've ever been on holiday with a lover and had drinks at a bar near a beach then you'll know the feeling I'm going for here.

"I want to make something scary that isn't all dark and stormy with vampires in it. Something scary in the sunshine."

"Good title."

"Thanks."

Bobby uses both hands in a gesture that's meant to represent words appearing on a screen or the bottom of a promotional poster. 'Sunny Florida – it's a scary place.' He smiles his smile at her and drinks again. See? He smiles a lot. He's likeable. "Actually, this whole country scares the shit out of me."

"Yeah, well, it's warmer."

"True, and I do like a warmer climate. But I still feel like a fish out of water here. Get it? Fish out of–"

"I'm serious. That movie scared the shit out of me when I was a kid."

"Yeah, when you were a kid. Now it's a rubber shark and a head rolling out of a wrecked boat."

"It's got good shots, good story."

"Good music."

"Good quotable lines."

"Good monologue." Bobby rolls his sleeve and points to a tattoo scar that isn't there and slurs, "'That's the USS Indianapolis'."

"Exactly. *And* it's scary."

"Which is what you want."

This time she toasts *his* point because it's accurate. She's drinking something in a classic martini glass to suggest she's cooler, not as frivolous, but still a drinker and therefore fun, like you and me maybe.

"So, scary summer film. With a shark."

She frowns and nods and says after a moment's thought, "Yeah, I'm thinking so."

"Okay."

"I like sharks."

"I know you do, baby." He smiles, and drinks.

"But we're not just throwing a load of pretty teenagers into the water to kill them off one by one."

"Heavens, no." He signals for a couple more drinks with one of those friendly gestures that says they come here often, theirs is a good marriage, and to prove it he takes her hand in his other one without even thinking about it.

"Although we'll have to have a significant number of deaths."

"Of course."

"And none of that false alarm scream crap either. None of that oh-my-God-it's-a-shark-but-no-it's-not-it's-my-boyfriend-messing-about-underwater crap. In fact, I want the *boy*friend screaming, fuck the girlfriend."

"Fuck the girlfriend?"

She gives him the look that couples have for each other when one of them is being silly at the wrong time.

"Because that's a different film entirely," he says anyway.

"It needs to be something different."

"Unless you mean he's screaming 'fuck the girlfriend'. Is that what you mean?"

The look has evolved into a look with raised eyebrows.

"A mutation maybe?" he says to compensate. "Genetic experiment?"

She wrinkles her nose at that.

"A feeding group brought close to the beach thanks to climate change."

"Too many, keep it simple."

"One big giant shark then."

"No, something *different*."

He raises his hands to the heavens in mock exasperation and then suggests "Vampire shark?"

"Keeping it real, remember."

"When so much in this business isn't."

"Exactly."

"*Open Water* tried to keep it real. And that sucked."

They both toast to that point, tipping their drinks back together.

*   *   *

RIGHT, BACK TO the movie business.

The good looking man slouched on a towel, reading from a sheet of paper clutched in one hand while a finger on his other hand follows the words, is an up-and-coming movie star. He moves his mouth when he reads, but to be fair to him he might be practising pronunciation or delivery or something else actors do. His name is immediately forgettable for now until you've seen it lots of times on posters and movie credits, something like Tom, Brad or Colin (but if you're thinking of another Tom, Brad or Colin currently working in the movie business then stop because he's younger and more surfer-dude type, and I only used those names in a Tom, Dick or Harry kind of way). Phil. That's his name. Probably Philip if he wants to be taken seriously, and he desperately does want to be taken seriously, although he never will be.

"Who's that?"

She only means to glance over to see who Bobby means but she lingers a little because although their marriage is good, the man on the towel reading his lines is a damn fine looking specimen of a man. "That's Phil."

"I mean, who is he in the film? I don't remember any surfer-types that actually have lines."

"He's our Dreyfus."

"Hardly."

"He's our shark expert. You know, our way of telling the audience things they need to know about sharks so they can be properly scared."

"Who isn't scared of sharks?"

She shrugs.

"Stop staring at him."

"But he's a damn fine looking specimen of a man."

"Bit too good looking for a shark expert, isn't he?"

"What, they're all ugly?"

He shrugs. "Anyway, sharks are on Discovery Channel all the time. People know it all already. And they've seen that movie. You know, that other one about a shark." He clicks his fingers, feigning memory loss.

"I think I'll change into my bikini."

"Don't you dare, or I'll change into one too."

"Gross."

"Gross is cutting open a shark and seeing everything spill out, like a fish head and a licence plate. Is the beautiful Phil going to do that, too?"

Sheila frowns at Bobby.

"You know, the autopsy scene? He pulls all that crap out of–"

"We're not just ripping off *Jaws*."

Bobby knows he's gone too far because they really aren't just ripping off *Jaws* and she's sensitive about that.

"Phil is actually Bodie," Sheila explains. (I know Bodie is a bit like Bobby but I'm trusting you won't get confused. It's also a bit like body, which might give your some idea of his role in this movie, and this story for that matter.)

"Okay," says Bobby (*not* Bodie) as he remembers the script.

"He was a surfer once until a narrow escape from a... tiger shark? Bull? Not sure. Anyway, he doesn't surf anymore but he's been obsessed with sharks ever since." She peers over the top of her sunglasses at her husband. "Maybe he watches Discovery Channel."

Bobby holds up both hands and backs away with that smile we've seen a few times already although this time it seems a little strained. And if this was a movie instead of a story, the bunch of girls in bikinis that come running in now would do it as part of the same shot, appearing behind him and running past with shrieks of laughter, giving us a smooth transition from him to them. They frolic in the shallows which is just about the only time you can ever use the word frolic (unless Sheila and Bobby were making a film about lambs in the spring, which they aren't). Bobby turns his head to watch them run by so when they splash each other and scoop up handfuls of water to throw, the view we have of them is his view.

"Hey!"

Sheila's voice brings us back to the director couple and she stabs at Bobby's eyes with forked fingers. He closes them and covers them with his hands and turns away before she can get him, not that she really would have.

"Good," she says, "Stay like that."

"But they're damn fine looking specimens."

"Shush."

He peers at her from between his fingers, probably smiling but we can't see that because of how his hands are up. What he sees is Sheila watching the girls kick water at each other and turn away shrieking. It's a sound she'll segue into a scream when they actually put it in the movie but for now they're getting too wet for a rehearsal.

"Girls, no nipples until we're rolling! Stay dry up there please!"

Sheila looks at Bobby and shrugs. "Gotta have something for the trailer."

"True. True."

"I figure we'll get a view inland from the jetty crane," she makes a sweeping gesture with her arms, "get them all frolicking with the store in shot behind them."

The store she means is actually a set. They've already filmed the inside shots at the studio, two couples buying supplies for a doomed fishing trip.

"Funny word," says Bobby. "Frolicking."

"We'll get that 'live bait' sign across the top of the shot, girls underneath."

"Subtle."

"After that, we'll kill them all."

Bobby claps his hands together and rubs them with maniacal glee. He's allowed to rub them with maniacal glee because this is a horror story about a horror film and I may never get the chance to use the expression again.

A LL RIGHT, REWIND again. Flashback.

"The shark's gotta be more than just a shark," says Sheila.

"Like I said, vampire shark."

"Asylum have done that already, surely."

"You're thinking Octoshark."

"Really?"

He shrugs, and drinks.

We're in the bar again. Same bar, same drinks, because it's the same conversation. I only ended it where I ended it before so you didn't get too bored reading the same scene and so I could end with that little dig at *Open Water*. It did suck, though.

"I mean it has to be a symbol, or a metaphor or something."

"Why? Isn't a thousand years of evolution into the perfect killing machine scary enough?"

"Scary, yeah, of course. I mean it's practically just muscle and teeth. But it needs to be something more if we aren't going straight to Blu-ray."

"Careful. Did you ever read *Jaws*?"

"Read it?"

"Yeah, the book. Quaint little things made of paper. People sometimes make movies out of them."

"Funny."

"The paper makes it easier to cut bits out."

"I know it's a book. I'm just surprised you do."

"Right."

"Peter Benchley."

"Now you're just showing off. All right, Benchley, whatever. Anyway, there was a metaphor in there that was *pretty fuck*ing lame."

In case you haven't read it, don't worry, because Sheila can't remember and Bobby has to explain.

"Out in the water you've got a lone shark, preying on the people of Amity, right? Is it still Amity in the book?"

"You're the expert."

"And on land, you've got a money lender bleeding the people dry. A *loan* shark. As in L, O, A, N."

"Really?"

"Really. As in really terrible."

They've got into the habit of toasting a good point, so Sheila does so here. "Well we should have something deeper than money anyway."

"Sex."

"I'm serious."

"Me too."

"I'd rather talk about the movie." She waggles her eyebrows like I'm told Groucho Marx does, or did, to show she's joking.

Bobby feigns disappointment by sticking out his lower lip, just going along with her joke because he loves her, then adds, "Big prehistoric phallic symbol of a shark."

She considers it, but, "I'd prefer vagina dentata."

"Why not both? Can it be both?"

"Oh *I* don't know."

Both of them slump in their seats, defeated for a moment. Thinking for a moment.

Bobby complains, "Why can't a monster just be a monster?" Then he blows bubbles into his drink with a straw.

It's a good point to end on for the moment, so let's go back, or rather forward…

…TO THE MOVIE. The movie stars, more precisely. They aren't being filmed right now but they are acting. Not too much emphasis on the acting, what they're doing is mostly natural, but they *are* acting a little bit.

We're with Phil and an actress called Brenda who we saw earlier splashing in the waves with her shrieking girly friends. Brenda was being Cassy then. They're not in role here, though. Phil is being Phil and Brenda Brenda and they're fucking each other in a crummy chalet room. They're still acting a bit though because each wants the other to think they're good at fucking, and each wants the other one to think that they think *they* are good at fucking, mainly so they can keep fucking on a regular basis for a while. For at least as long as it takes to make the film anyway.

They are both naked. It's all very well lit. Phil is sitting on the bed and Brenda has straddled him, bouncing in his lap at a speed that must be bringing him close, or her close, whoever – the main thing is, we're joining them at a critical moment. She's bouncing, ponytail hair whipping around behind her, with one arm draped around Phil's neck and the other groping at his pectoral muscles which is fair because one of his hands is on her chest too, holding one breast then the other as if trying to stop them bouncing too much. His other hand is at the small of her back so she doesn't fall off the bed, or more importantly so she doesn't fall off of him. She is making a lot of noise because she wants him to think he's good and she wants him to like how much she likes it so they can keep doing this for a while, and before this movie she did some others she's not so proud of so she knows how to make those noises pretty good. Phil is giving her an occasional "oh yeah" so she knows it's working.

You get the picture. Young, damn fine looking specimens enjoying the fact that they are young damn fine looking specimens.

They near climax, and it's bound to have happened perfectly together if not for this interruption. The door to the room bursts open suddenly with the same shocking force their orgasm might have had, had it been allowed, but instead we're going to have a climax of a different sort because, let's face it, there hasn't been any blood yet and a horror film tends to need some. Not always, some of the best ones don't have any, but this is the movie business, albeit the budget movie business, and in the budget horror movie business blood is something they can always afford to use. Besides, they're having sex, so death is sure to follow. It's still the rules, even if *Scream* told you that already.

Brenda turns, surprised, and for a moment her breasts are free of Phil's hand so we get a tantalising glimpse of both of them together. Phil gives a manly, "What the hell are you doing here?" which tells us whoever has come in is someone he knows but if it were a film they would not be in shot. As it's a story I can even have the intruder speak and you still won't know who it is.

"No wonder there's been no chemistry."

And Brenda screams, and so does Phil.

YOU MUST HAVE a good idea who it might have been; there aren't many characters to choose from. Unless it's someone new but that wouldn't be fair at this point, would it. Bit like cheating. So let me just say you're right, and move on with the story.

Bobby and Sheila are watching Phil and Brenda on a monitor. Nothing kinky – it's footage from earlier in the week, not the sex scene from the motel. The sex you just read hasn't actually happened yet, this is another flashback.

Phil is being Bodie and Brenda is being Cassy and they are sitting on the raft we saw right at the beginning. Cassy is lying on her back, sunning herself, in a tiny white bikini because white is pure and virginal (though Brenda isn't) and she is going to be one of the survivors (though Brenda isn't). Phil is sitting next to her, glistening because he's just been in the water and because the reflected light gives his torso more muscle definition. If all had gone well, this would have been the poster shot for the movie, with an added fin circling the raft.

"You know, there was a shark attack here last year," says Phil who is Bodie to Brenda who is Cassy.

She sits up, but not entirely. Just enough that we can see she has a flat stomach and perfect breasts. She is propped up on her forearms and elbows, which pushes her chest out more. She knew to do this without direction because of the films she's made before.

"You're kidding."

Bodie (you know it's really Phil pretending to be Bodie so I'll stop saying so) he shakes his head without looking at Cassy. "They like the warm climate." He's looking out to sea.

"Bodie, are you trying to scare me?"

"No."

"Because there are other ways to keep me on this raft, you know."

("You see," says Sheila, pointing back and forth between the characters on the screen, "There's supposed to be some chemistry here. Some sexual tension. We've got nothing.")

Bodie glances at Cassy and she smiles a dazzling smile that is nearly as white as her pure virginal bikini and he says, "It's true." It's a deliberately ambiguous reply because it's true that there are other ways to keep her on the raft, but also it's true that there was a shark attack here, the audience has already seen it in the film. We're meant to wonder if we'll see another one in a minute, or if we'll get the kissing and groping Cassy seems to be hinting at. Either way the audience would be happy, most likely. What they get instead, though, is backstory and shark info.

"They'll eat anything, you know. Turtles, tin cans. Surfers."

("But probably not your meatloaf," says Bobby and Sheila slaps his arm without looking at him, looking only at the screen. "This is shite," she says. It's a Britishism she likes.)

Cassy sits up fully now, and the close-up is of their faces together. It's going to be one of *those* moments, where lead characters get closer emotionally as well as physically. The movement also tells the audience this is going to be important information.

"They've got these jagged teeth, triangle teeth, and not just the one row. There are lots of teeth. They shed them and replace them all the time. And when it comes at you, its jaw drops open all the way down, like, ninety degrees, and all you can see is teeth and darkness."

Cassy puts her hand on Bodie's arm, squeezes his bicep.

"You know, when it's got you, a shark will just roll, left and right. Waving its pectoral fins. The water resistance keeps you from moving much but the shark can move, and its teeth cut back and forth like a chainsaw."

"Oh, Bodie..."

He looks at her then, pulled out of his memory, and gives her a weak smile. Then they kiss. Then they lay back. They kiss again. Cassy's hand is on Bodie's thigh. As she caresses him, his shorts rise up and we can see the beginning of a bite scar there.

("This is meant to be tentative," says Sheila. "They're kissing for the first time, she's kissing for the first time *ever* actually, but here…" and because they're married and they finish each other's sentences sometimes, Bobby says, "Here she looks like a college slut." "Yeah," says Sheila, "She might as well just go right for his cock.")

As they lay kissing, a fin rises up out of the water briefly, passes, and is gone.

Sheila hits the pause button so all there is on-screen is dark water.

"And that was take a hundred or whatever."

"I thought they were messing it up on purpose. Get a little more kissy-kissy." Bobby gropes an imaginary woman in front of him.

"They're killing my movie."

"Our movie, baby."

"We'll have to re-shoot it."

Except they can't, because Phil and Brenda, who are the Bodie and Cassy they need for the scene, for the rest of the film in fact, will be dead soon.

But then you already knew that.

THE CHALET DOOR is open and the bed sheets are tangled and there is blood everywhere. There's blood everywhere because there isn't a body to hold it all anymore, not exactly. Both bodies are here, but they're in pieces. Blood has soaked the bed, the floor, and it splashes up the walls in long lines. There's even an arc of it across the ceiling.

The man standing in the doorway is wearing a blazer, despite the heat, but no tie. His shirt is a grubby white because he's a good guy but not too squeaky clean. He is looking over the scene calmly, hands in his pockets. He's clearly a cop, even though he's not in uniform and there's no gun visible or anything. He just is, and you can tell just by looking.

"Sir? You can't be in here."

A patrolman stands near. He reaches for the man, then reaches for his gun when the other man reaches inside his blazer.

"Steady," says the man in the blazer we know is a cop. He produces a flip-fold ID. He shows it upside down, realises, and turns it the right way. A little detail. It keeps us with the photo and the police badge for a moment. See, he's a cop.

"Sorry Sir."

"New?"

"Two weeks, Sir."

In any other story, that would mark him as a dead-man-to-be. Not this one. He's not in the story anymore, except for his arm in a moment, and the arm is still attached to his body when that happens.

The detective steps further into the room and looks around so we can see again the bloody horror of it all. So much blood. And chunks. Occasionally there's a piece you might recognise, like an elbow or a few toes still connected.

"Let us through," comes Sheila's voice from outside.

"Ma'am," says someone else, "Stop." Our two-week-old patrolman.

The man who is a detective glances behind at the noise briefly, then squats down and tilts his head to look under the bed. It means the doorway is free behind him to frame a good shot of Sheila and Bobby together as they stand on the threshold, held back by the arm of the patrolman. Sheila brings her hand up to her mouth, either to stifle a scream or hold back vomit. Bobby says, "Bloody hell."

"Bloody," says the cop, reaching under the bed with a pen. "You got that right."

"What happened?"

Bobby's question is a stupid question in the general sense, but in the specific actually quite interesting.

The cop brings something out from under the bed using his pen. It is triangular and jagged.

"If I didn't know any better," says the cop, "I'd say it was a shark attack."

It's too early to say so, of course, but it saves writing a post-mortem scene. Besides, this is the CSI generation. He should have figured out the whole case by now.

*   *   *

"WHAT ARE WE going to do now? We can't just re-cast both of them."

"Just one, then."

Sheila thinks about it. The day of filming has been cancelled, so they're sitting on set in the sun. The set they're sitting on is the raft because it keeps people from coming over and asking questions. They can see everybody else, the crew, the cops, the reporters, back on the beach.

"He said shark attack."

"Yeah."

"On land. Interesting."

"Yeah. Shame we're not making a film about making a film about a shark attack, it could have been a good scene."

"Original."

Bobby dips his foot into the water, likes the temperature, and puts both feet in. Sheila is laying back, propped up on her elbows. Her bikini is black and oily looking because it's wet. She is thinking about how to fix the film but Bobby is thinking about her bikini and how he'd like to take it off but figures that might be a bit weird after what just happened. And anyway, they'd have an audience. Not you, so much, but the people on the beach. Sheila and Bobby don't know about you, this isn't *that* kind of story.

"The scene where Bodie looks out to sea with his arm around his surfboard."

"What about it?"

"Well, instead of having him turn around and walk back inland, another failed attempt to get back surfing, we could just cut it with him looking. We could put that in *after* the raft scene instead, which we already have–"

"Without chemistry."

"Without chemistry. And then that can be his last scene. Looking out to sea, surfboard in the sand beside him, arm around it like a lover."

"There was more chemistry between him and the surfboard."

"We don't see him again, but we do see the surfboard. It washes up on the beach—"

"—with a big bite out of it."

"Exactly."

"Emotional."

"Yeah. He finally kisses Cassy, having told his story, gets some closure of sorts, and that's it."

"Meanwhile, Cassy the virgin never-kissed-anyone feels like it's her fault."

"Yeah."

"Except we don't have a Cassy anymore. And too many shots with her and Bodie together to simply re-shoot."

Bobby kicks his feet in the water. He's not worried about how a shark can detect minute disturbances in the water with its lateral line sensory system. He knows about it, he just isn't worried about it. Neither is Sheila. She drapes one hand into the cool water as she thinks about how they can fix their movie.

"Bobby? Sheila?"

The voice comes from the radio Bobby has clipped to his shorts. They didn't swim out – they came in a small motorboat.

"Ignore him."

"It's Tony," Bobby explains, "You know how he gets." He unclips the radio and says, "Yeah, Tony, Bobby."

"We got a dwarf here wants to speak to you."

"Did you say dwarf?"

"Midget, then. Vertically challenged. Whatever. Says he was in *Jaws*. Says he's come to see you."

"Shit," says Sheila, "I totally forgot about him."

"Dwarf?" says Bobby again, this time to Sheila.

"Little person, for the cage scenes with the real shark. To make it look bigger."

"Oh."

She makes a 'gimme gimme' gesture for the radio and he hands it over.

"Hi Tony, Sheila. We'll come get him."

"Roger that."

Sheila sighs. "At least out here nobody *else* will bother us."

Bobby puts his hand on his wife's knee and tries his smile. It nearly works. "We'll get through this."

There's another burst from the radio.

"Bobby? Sheila?"

"Tony, yeah, what?"

"There's someone here to see you."

"A dwarf, yeah, we know, keep your panties on. We're coming to get him."

"No, not him. A cop. Says it's important."

Bobby looks at Sheila who says, "Fuck it, bring him out here too."

Bobby looks at their tiny outboard and says, "We're gonna need a bigger–"

"Don't. Don't say it."

THE COP WANTS to talk to Bobby and Sheila about some film footage. Not theirs, though.

"You got somewhere I can play this?" he says to them as they pull their boat up onto the sand. He shows them a video cassette.

"Not here," says Bobby, "We use digital."

"What is it?" asks Sheila.

"I'd rather just show you," he says. "Let you clear something up for me."

So far, so Columbo.

Sheila shrugs. "There's a player in the warehouse set."

"Warehouse?" The cop looks around but there's no warehouse here.

"Warehouse *set*," Sheila says. She points at the bait shop they'd used earlier. "It's different inside."

So they head over. Tony approaches with a small guy you only know as the dwarf or midget or vertically challenged man from *Jaws*.

"Later, Tony," says Bobby. "Something needs clearing up first."

Bobby doesn't sound like Columbo when he says it. He sounds more like the godfather or something.

Inside, the set is empty. There's no shooting today. The warehouse is all old looking boards and crates. In the middle of the room, though, is a large fish tank. As in the tank is large, but also as in it could hold a large fish. Both definitions apply. Anyway, beside this is the video player and a small TV and a few plastic chairs.

"What's all this?" He's a cop. He's naturally curious.

"We got a guy with a baby shark in these scenes. He's filming it, studying it. Feeding it. Lets us show the audience how a shark feeds in close-up detail that won't bring the rating up or get us censored. It's also why people keep getting killed, the parents have come for it and are terrorising the beach."

"Parents, huh?"

"Yeah, there's two. Only you'll never see both together. One will get killed and you'll think it's safe and then wham, here's the other one. It's like our twist."

The cop peers in. "Where's the shark?"

Bobby and Sheila exchange a glance.

"We don't have one."

"It'll be rubber or CGI or paper mâché or something," Bobby explains.

"But it'll look real enough."

"Oh."

"So what's the tape?"

The cop, let's call him Travis, pops the tape into the machine and says, "You tell me."

There's no need for anyone to tell him anything, it's clear immediately what it is. It's security footage of the parking lot of the chalet motel where many of the actors are staying. It doesn't play continuous footage but a sequence of stills taken at intervals. And here. Comes. A car. Parking. In the next shot the door is suddenly open. And here's–

Bobby.

"You went to the motel?"

Bobby looks at Sheila who is frowning. She even takes a step back away from him.

"Yeah," Bobby says. He says it somewhat reluctantly. Then again to the cop. Travis. "Yeah. I did."

"Why?"

"I just wanted to talk to her." Bobby says this to Sheila. Her arms are crossed and her frown has deepened.

"She wasn't alone, though, was she," says Travis.

"No."

"One of the other guests heard an argument."

"That's right. I wasn't, *we* wasn't, we *weren't*, happy with one of their scenes. I told them so."

"And then what?"

"Not what *you* think."

"And what do I think?"

"That the next thing I did was kill them."

"Actually, no. If I thought that, we'd be doing this downtown, as they say in the movies. The only screams I got from this neighbour are the 'get the fuck out' kind, and look." He points at the screen and Bobby's car is. One shot. At a time. Leaving the lot. Too soon for him to have done much of anything.

"Oh."

"So?"

"Well, the next thing was Cassy quit."

"You mean Brenda?"

"Yeah. She said she didn't like having a pervert director and could earn more doing other films."

"Weird," says Sheila.

"Why's that?" asks Travis.

Sheila looks at him and says, "Well I've seen her other films."

Travis looks like he wants to ask something, then doesn't, then does, but this time it's probably different to what he wanted to ask. He's a cop.

He can figure out the films Brenda used to make for himself. "Then what happened?" is what he says to Bobby.

"Bodie quit too. Phil. Moral support I think. I left them to it, figuring they'd cool down and change their minds in the morning."

"Is that all?" Sheila says.

"Yes."

So she says it again to Travis. "Is that all?" and gestures to the empty parking lot on the screen to emphasise her point.

"Not quite. Hold on."

They wait.

"I'd fast forward only I'd probably miss it and then we'd have to rewind again and it's easier if – here we go."

And here it is. Another. Car. Parking.

Sheila's.

Sheila shows Bobby her palms and says, "I just wanted to talk to him."

"Wasn't there though, was he," says Bobby.

"No."

"Because he was with Cass– with *Brenda*."

"Well I know that *now*, yeah."

Travis, the cop, feels he should ask another question or two because he is, after all, the cop. "The question I have for you both is this…"

Both of them wait a moment.

"Any ideas who'd want them dead?"

ALL RIGHT, NEARLY finished.

You hear that? Of course you don't. You'll have to imagine it. Imagine a soundtrack that sounds a bit like *Jaws* even though it's trying really hard not to. An underwater moving shot along the ocean bed, coming up to where the sun dapples the surface of the water, glinting and sparkling. Cut into this brightness with the sleek dark body not of a shark but the underside of a boat. No mini motorboat this time but a proper big vessel. Not too big, as you'll see as we come up out of the water, just big enough for a small crew and a shark cage and a dwarf. Okay, so the dwarf doesn't need much room, but he's there too so I need to mention him. The dwarf is Manny and he's definitely a dwarf and not a midget. He's not the guy they used in *Jaws* by the way, he just says he is to get more work. No one ever checks.

"Okay, okay, this will do."

Bobby has to shout it because he's at the front of the boat looking in the water.

"You sure? We're not very far out." This comes from the boat owner, Smith. He knows the front of the boat is really called the bow but he's not writing this story. He's dressed as if he's going to be in the movie; woollen sweater, tatty at the seams, a baseball cap with anchor insignia, shorts stained with fish-gut, sandals. He's not in the movie. He's not even in the story for much longer, and he certainly doesn't have any more dialogue.

"He's sure," says Sheila. "He has a good sense for these things." She gives the thumb-to-finger okay signal to her husband up front as Smithy kills the engine.

"I feel ridiculous."

Manny is fidgeting with what look to be breasts but is actually a stuffed sports bra he has on underneath his wetsuit. Some of the crew laugh again. They've laughed at him a lot.

"You're Cassy," Sheila reminds him, "troubled teenager, anxious to face the shark that took the man you loved."

"I'm Cassy. Right."

"Well, from a distance."

Sheila thinks that for the close-ups they'll get one of the girls to wear the mask and be all wide-eyed with fright. She figures she may even have the girl spit out the respirator in panic so her underwater screams and the released oxygen give them a lot of bubbles to obscure things. And they'll tear the suit in such a way that as she swims away she's pretty much naked flesh and breasts so no one will notice the body double.

"You sure you wanna do this?" Bobby asks.

"Yeah, no problem," says Manny, which is a bit embarrassing because Bobby was talking to Sheila. "Oh."

"Yeah, we don't have much choice but to kill her off now do we," she says.

Neither of them pay much heed to the fact she has been killed once already, for real. This is showbiz.

"I hear your girl got herself murdered," says Manny. He's stepping into the cage now, breasts and all. It's a specially adapted cage, smaller than the usual.

"Sort of," Bobby admits. He has come down to help.

"Shark attack," says Sheila.

"Huh?" is as much as Manny can protest because Sheila calls to the winch guy and Manny-Cassy is hauled up into the air and over the side of the boat. He would like to call, "Wait!" and get some more details about the shark attack but he's already being lowered and he needs to breathe so he puts the respirator in his mouth instead and disappears into the deep blue sea.

"Dinner is served."

"Roll cameras."

Bobby announces, "Time to chum the waters," and returns to the front of the boat where a couple of tubs wait for him. Each is filled with fish heads and tails and guts in a soup of blood and scales. Bobby has a trowel in his hand and he shovels the stuff into the water. It's sloppy splashy work, and smelly too. Look as one scoop of blood and chunks is slung over the side: sploosh! And another scoop that looks already chewed: sploop! And this one, red-wet and blood-slick, is an open flip-fold ID with a police badge and picture we know better upside down and without all the blood...

Splash!

So what happened to the cop?

Well, you know what happened. He's dead. But what actually happened, what are the details?

He wanted to talk to Bobby and Sheila, remember? He wanted to talk to them about some film footage. And after that he asked if they had any idea who might have killed them. (Of course they did, but they weren't going to say so.) Well after *that* he said he wanted to shut them down.

"The thing is, it could be any one of your cast or your crew, and if it isn't we're still gonna need to talk to all of them. It'll take a while."

Bobby stands. "Out of the question, chum."

Travis looks at Sheila with raised eyebrows. She shrugs and says, "He's British," by way of explanation.

"Your two main characters are dead, how are you still filming anyway?"

"They *were* the main characters. Now they're bit parts."

Sheila stands beside her husband. "We evolve."

"And evolution never stops."

"Well, this movie does." Travis stands up too. He ejects the video cassette. "For a little while, anyway. Sorry."

"If we stop filming the movie will die."

"Like a shark, huh?"

"This movie is our baby."

Travis looks from one to the other. He wants to touch his gun, just for the reassurance, but he doesn't because that would be silly because this man is a British film director and this one's a woman in a bikini, and anyway he has the video tape in his gun hand.

"What's going on here?"

"A ruthless business," says Sheila.

"Cutthroat, really," Bobby agrees.

"It'll chew you up and spit you out if you're not careful."

Finally beginning to see the significance of their comments, Travis glances at the cassette tape in his hand.

"We went back later," Sheila explains. "Together. Parked down the street."

Travis swaps hands with the tape and goes for his gun but Bobby is already smiling at him and there are *a lot* of teeth in that smile. A lot.

"What *are* you?"

Bobby's mouth is open. It has expanded for all the teeth, so many teeth, too many teeth. They snap together as he tries to speak.

"Shust a monshter."

"What?" Travis asks Sheila. It's a pretty big question that could simply be an abbreviated repeat of what are you, or what is he, or it could be what shall I do, or maybe it's all he can manage of a good plain what the fuck.

Sheila chooses to think of it as what did he say and answers accordingly.

"He's trying to say, 'just a monster'."

It shouldn't be a surprise to you, there were plenty of clues. I mean, I mentioned his teeth a lot, and his smile. Plus there was that 'fish out of water' line near the beginning, and that 'warmer climate' reference. A few others. And shame on you if you thought it was the shark man from the beginning, the one with the fake fin, because I told you he wasn't in it again.

There's a tearing sound as Bobby's fin, a very real fin, splits the fabric of his shirt. But like I said, you shouldn't be surprised.

Travis, the cop, the symbol of law and order in a world that's just gone all messed-up otherworldly, *is* surprised. He's not used to this. He's used to the butler did it, or a jealous mistress. So faced with a man with an elongating head, a greying head, a head with an open maw of teeth and receding beard, Travis can only stand paralysed. He thinks it has to be a special effect or something, and he has a goofy smile on his face when he looks at Sheila to say, "All right, joke's over."

But Sheila says, "You know what scares me most about *Jaws?*"

Travis can only shake his head, but it might be in disbelief rather than as an answer.

"It's that such a magnificent creature was stopped by an everyday seaside cop." Her eyes are fully black now, as oily dark as her swimsuit. "The joke's not over until you smile, you sonofabitch." She shows him how. Then her own mouth stretches and opens, opens, as it fills with teeth, lots of teeth, so many many teeth.

It shouldn't be a surprise to you, there were plenty of clues. I mean, there's the twist in their own film, for one thing, with the two sharks and their baby and all. And look at the title; it's not just Shark! is it, it's 'Shark! Shark!'. (I was going to go with 'Somewhere, Beyond the Scene' but a pun sets the wrong tone, don't you think? Like this is a funny story or something, and not serious horror.)

Travis can only watch, gun useless in one hand and video tape in the other, as the husband and wife step closer. They'll eat anything, even a cop, especially if it threatens their movie.

Sheila's jaw is hanging right down to her chest now, impossibly large and open, and Bobby's is the same. If this were a film then one of them would come right at you, quick, an extreme close-up down the throat as the jaws close and the screen goes suddenly black.

Imagine that in 3D.

BACK ON THE BOAT, Bobby is still scooping a bloody swill of chum into the sea. Evidence, really, but some genuine fish chum too.

"How's the little guy doing?" Sheila asks her crew. The camera crew, not the boat crew.

While everyone's attention is on the cross-dressing dwarf, Bobby scoops a handful of bloody guts from the barrel and tucks it quickly into his mouth.

"How we doing up there?" Sheila shouts to him.

He wipes his mouth clean and scoops the next lot overboard like he's supposed to.

"Getting hungry," he says, thinking maybe she saw him.

"As soon as we've got some shots of our fishy friends we'll break for lunch."

She shouts it to everyone but Bobby knows better: she saw him for sure.

He turns to the ocean, shovelling chum and eager for the promised break, calling, "Shark! Shark!"

- Fin -

Roll credits. (Rock music optional.)

ABOUT THE AUTHOR

Ray Cluley is a writer. It used to be that he was a teacher who *said* he was a writer, but now it's actually true. His stories have appeared in various dark places, such as *Black Static, Crimewave,* and *Interzone* from TTA Press, *Shadows & Tall Trees* from Undertow Books, and various anthologies and podcasts. A novelette with Spectral Press is due in 2014, and a collection (*Probably Monsters*) with ChiZine Press is due in 2015. His stories 'At Night, When the Demons Come' and 'Bones of Crow' were selected by Ellen Datlow for her *Best Horror of the Year* anthology, and 'Night Fishing' was selected by Steve Berman for *Wilde Stories 2013,* while 'Beachcombing' has been translated into French for *Ténèbres 2011.* 'Shark! Shark!' recently won the British Fantasy Award for Best Short Story (2013). He writes non-fiction too, but generally he prefers to make stuff up.

Lightning Source UK Ltd.
Milton Keynes UK
UKOW04f0623280914

239289UK00006B/74/P